TREE FROG AND HER HONEY BADGER

A FUC ACADEMY STORY

JULIA MILLS

AUTHOR'S NOTE

Hey, y'all! Thank you so much for reading my book. I cannot properly express how amazing it is to be writing a story in Eve Langlais' World.

I have been a fan of hers since before I ever dreamed of publishing my own stories. Her amazing characters and inventive worlds have transported me to places I never knew possible. To be a part of the action, a small cog in this fantastic machine, well, it is simply a dream come true.

I sure hope you enjoy Tree Frog and Her Honey Badger and all the stories in this amazing EveL world, created by the one and only Eve Langlais.

Stay safe. Take care. And ALWAYS dare to dream.

XOXO, Julia

ACKNOWLEDGMENTS

Line edits by Devin Govaere

Proofread by Book Nook Nuts

Beta Read by Charlene Bauer, Linda Levy, and Beverley Pritchard

Cover by Rebecca Poole with Dreams2Media

To Liz and Em, you are my world. Beautiful women, inside and out who make every day a blessing. I am so proud of you.

To all the men and women in service in every country of the world—thank you for all you do.

To Jess Ripley – Lady, you are amazing. Thank you for everything you do for all of us and for ALWAYS being a bright spot in my day! YOU ARE A ROCK STAR!

INTRODUCTION

The world has gone mad! Absolutely nuckin' futs crazy!
Well, maybe not *yet*, but Dr. Winifred—please call her
Freddie—Lightfoot is sure all hell's about to break loose if
she doesn't stop the idiot who's destroying the world's
coffee fields.

Life *without* caffeine is a no-go for this FUC superhero. A
world without her favorite drink is not a world she wants
to live in. Time to throw on her rainbow wings and kick
tail, even if it means putting off meeting a certain sexy-as-
the-day-is-long honey badger.

Retirement was boring. Buck Blackthorne needed adven-
ture, purpose, and to be on the front lines again. One
quick email to Furry United Coalition Newbie Academy
—FUCN'A—and everything was a go.
With more years of combat under his belt than all the
cadets combined, he just knew training would be a snap!

Well, like a *bang, boom, kapow* and a trip to the infirmary…
on second thought, maybe retirement wasn't so bad.

But one whiff of a certain sexy winged tree frog and all
bets were off. He was in for the long haul and ready to
claim her as his own… But where the hell did she go?
One unanswered phone call, a supersonic trip south, and
jumping from a perfectly good plane was all in a day's
work for this honey badger hero. There wasn't a jungle
that could stop him, but prehistoric shifters? Well, that
was a new one.

Time to save his mate, save the day, and, heaven help him,
save the coffee! Oh, baby, put your head between your
legs and kiss your booty goodbye. Time to get FUC'd in
the best possible way.

Does this premise and world seem familiar? That's because it is based off the Eve
Langlais Furry United Coalition. Eve Langlais has invited her author friends to come
and play in her world. To find out more, visit Worlds.EveLanglais.com.

"Well, hell, Buck," his little sister grumbled, crossing her arms over her chest and furrowing her brows. He was pretty sure she even added a *harrumph* before going on. "If I'd known you wanted to go into law enforcement, I could've put in a good word for you at the Agency. We could've worked together. Just like old times. Like here at the bar, only we wouldn't have had to clean up messes and Mom isn't there to tell us what to do."

"Yeah, I know." He tried not to sound ungrateful for the offer. It wasn't that he didn't want to work with his sister. Heck, they were family, and in the Blackthorne clan, that meant everything. It was just that... that... "I really wanted to do this on my own, sis. Ya know?"

"I heard *that*, Miss Missy," came the immediate gruff rebuke from Janice, his mom, the leader of their honey badger clan. Not anywhere near done, the owner of the renowned Sundowner—the largest and most popular paranormal bar in the whole southern half of the U.S.— grumbled, her index finger pointing right at his sister.

"Workin' with me is a pleasure. I'm a damned delight every minute of every day, and you know it."

"Yeah, Mom." Shauna sighed, without the slightest attempt at being subtle with her sarcasm. "You're a number one, top of the list…"

"Queen of the hill," Buck's youngest brother, Jack, chimed in, singing the rest of "New York, New York" in the background.

Ignoring everything else but making her point, as was the usual, Janice pointed out, "And you know that your brother's always been that way. Always had to do things for himself. Never wants anyone's help. Hell, he demanded to be born a month early, kicking and screaming, ready to get a move on, not even giving your daddy or me time to call the midwife."

Shaking her head and chuckling, she added, "He walked before he crawled at five months old and had a black eye ten minutes later."

Winking in his direction, Buck's mom turned back to his sister, not missing a beat or taking a breath. "Shauna, my girl, you know damned good and well every single one of your brothers is the same way. They get the stubbornness from your daddy's side. God rest his soul. They just gotta do every damned thing the hard way."

Her chuckles getting louder, the honey badger matriarch added, "Usually through the mud, the muck, and the blood."

"You are so right, Momma, I wholeheartedly agree." Shauna nodded like one of those bobblehead dogs in the back of Old Lady Simpson's bubble-gum pink 1959 Cadillac Eldorado.

"Can you help a guy out?" Buck asked Abe, his brother-in-law, a revered Dragon Guardsmen and member of the Dragon Protection Agency—another super-secret, protect-the-world-but-stay-hidden, and deal-with-the-shit-nobody-else-can Agency that only took the best of the best from the paranormal community. Abe was a true warrior, inside and out. "I mean, I know Shauna is your mate and all, but, daaaaaamn. Throw a guy a bone. We're bros. You're supposed to have my back."

The dragon they all called a Hell's Angels' Reject because he was big, bald, bad to the bone, heavily tattooed, and rode an extra-large Harley Fat Boy, chuckled, snaked his arm around Shauna, pulled her close, and laid a kiss atop her head. "Son, I know which side my bread is buttered on..."

"And he knows what the couch feels like if he pisses me off," Buck's sister growled before giving in and letting out the chuckle that already had her shoulders bouncing up and down.

"Wow, sis," Spencer, the second male in the Blackthorne family pecking order, yelped as he entered the backside of the bar carrying two cases of Corona and one of Jack Daniels. "You women are so cold. Go straight for the kill. Know you got us guys right where you want us. Y'all are scary. Hope to hell my mate never finds me."

"Yeah, right." Abe's low rumbling laugher filled the empty bar. "You say that now, but just wait till she's close. You get that first whiff of something so sweet, so wonderful that you just wanna find her, pick her up, and throw her over your shoulder and head for the hills." Pausing to take a quick breath, his laughter getting the best of him, the Guardsman nodded with wide eyes. "Listen up, kid. I know what I'm talkin' 'bout. Your sister had me tied around her finger from the get-go."

Kissing Shauna's cheek, Abe winked. "And that's exactly where I wanted to be. Still do."

Buck couldn't help but roll his eyes as Shauna and Abe did the whole "lookin' into each other's eyes" thing that lovers—especially shifters—did. It was sickening in the best of times and downright obnoxious as of late.

Yeah, well, it's 'cause you're trying to hide the fact that you met your own sweet little mate that it pisses you off so badly....

Yep, it was true. There was no denying it. He could damn sure try to hide it, especially from his family, but facts were facts, and they were staring him right in the face.

Buck Blackthorne was the biggest, roughest, toughest honey badger the world had ever known—at least in his own mind. He was eldest child and the first son of Janice and Henry Buck Blackthorne. He was a highly decorated Marine in more conflicts and wars than he cared to count.

Yet even he was vulnerable to being bit by the mating bug. His coarse-pelted ass had walked right into the Furry United Coalition Newbie Academy—FUCN'A for those in the know—and within a week found his one and only mate.

He'd been in the middle of his first solo demonstration in his favorite class—Advanced Explosives—showing the cadets how to make a bomb out of a can of beer, a pair of lady's silk skivvies, and a paper clip. Then that shit blew right up in his face.

That crap had never happened. Not in all the years he

served as a Marine and was deployed to every country worldwide. Not once when he used that very device to get rid of moles— not the shifter kind, the bratty kind that got off being pains in the ass in his mom's garden. Not even when he'd taught Shauna how to make the device to impress her buddies at the Agency.

Nope, had never happened before that day. Not even in a foxhole in a desert on the other side of the world with bombs exploding on one side, gunfire on the other, and a tank full of the enemy about to crawl up his ass. Nope, Buck was the picture of cool under pressure, assembling three identical bombs in ninety-two-and-a-half seconds, lighting their fuses, and making it to cover before the first grain of sand was flying through the air.

Shame he hadn't been so lucky in his debut at FUCN'A...

It was a shitshow from the very beginning. A few seconds in, he dropped the paperclip and kicked it across the room to parts unknown. At ten seconds on the dot, he was supposed to attach a thin thread he'd torn off the waistband of the panties to the tab on the top of the beer can and snapped that son of a bitch right off. Shit, couldn't even drink the beer that way. Not without shotgunning the SOB, and who shotgunned cheap beer?

Frat boys, maybe? Damned sure not me.

But did he stop? Ask for a do-over? Request being moved to the end of the line so he could take a breath before starting over?

No. No. And no.

Instead, the never-say-die, too-cocky-for-his-own-good honey badger kept right on going. So, at thirty-one seconds on the stopwatch, nine seconds ahead of schedule, when he lit the fuse—aka the crotch of the panties, twisted tight—and the damned thing blew up right in his face, Buck wasn't really surprised. Pissed and embarrassed, but not surprised.

Laughing their asses off, his fellow cadets were merciless in their creative teasing and inventive names, his favorite being Blown-Out Badger. Hell, he didn't blame them. Had the boot been on the other paw, Buck would've done the same thing. He'd have been leading the chant, more than likely up on a desk, beating his hands on the ceiling for effect.

To his credit, Professor Matthew Firestone—a dragon shifter with one hell of a sense of humor and a good friend of his brother-in-law's—worked really hard to keep a straight face and didn't flunk him on the spot. Nope, Firestone was super cool. Even gave Buck extra credit for "courage and perseverance under fire."

All of that should've been enough to make Buck rethink all his plans, but there was more. He'd been covered from head-to-toe in nasty, boiling Pabst Blue Ribbon beer, the stench that emanated from his very pores smelling worse than the bathrooms at the Sundowner the day after the all-night Schnedeker Skunk's Family Mating Party. Any sensible person would have, at the very least, taken the day off. But bowing in the face of defeat was for cowards, and no Blackthorne *anywhere* had ever been called a coward.

Crazy? For sure. Stupid? The males, after too much whiskey. But never, ever, a coward.

He tried to laugh it off as he pulled pieces of aluminum

can from the stubble covering his jaw, the exposed skin of his arms, and way too close to the family jewels on the front of the crotch of his pants and both of his thighs. Matt Firestone demanded he see the Academy doctor, even though Buck's honey badger was already working to repair the plethora of gashes, cuts, scrapes, and burns. All Buck could do was blow out an extremely exasperated breath and head to the infirmary.

Climbing the stairs of the Academy was the first time he'd stopped to ask himself if he was doing the right thing. From one step to the next, he started seriously contemplating going back to the lovely, quiet retirement he'd been enjoying since leaving the Marines.

Stepping onto the main floor, he unconsciously made an immediate right. Three steps toward the clinic, lost in thought, Buck was damned near bowled over by the scent of fresh, clean moss just like the swamp right out his backdoor. Inhaling deeper, he caught a whiff of ozone, the clean aroma that filled the air right after a lightning strike. As if that wasn't enough, the whole wonderful perfume was topped off with the citrusy scent of verbena. It was the best thing he'd ever smelled, and dadgummit, his honey badger was right there with him.

Pushing against the inside of his skin, doing his damnedest to jump right out into the open and make his presence known, that badger was hot on the trail of something good. And, well, so was Buck's cock.

Jumping to attention, pushing against the zipper of his camos so hard he was sure the zigzag design would be there forever, it took all of his considerable control not to sprint down the hall. Walking slowly, counting his steps, and trying hard not to draw attention to himself, Buck's eyes slid side to side.

It was a covert mission of the highest order. She—that elusive creature known as his mate—was somewhere close by. She had to be. No other scent could make both man and badger stand at attention.

"Where is she? I know she's here. Why can't we find her?"

"Hell, if I know," Harry, the honey badger with whom Buck shared his soul, growled. *"If you'd have let me outta here ten seconds ago, we'd already have found her, have her naked, and be having our wicked way with her."*

"Yeah, okay, Casanova," Buck grumbled. *"Save it for somebody who doesn't know you."*

"Like you're any better. Do you even remember the last time you got laid?" Not waiting for an answer, the surly, old honey badger snarled, *"Nope, neither do I. You need—"*

"I need you to shut the hell up," Buck snapped, slamming his mental shields tight as he opened the door to the infirmary.

Instantly engulfed in a heavenly fog of the same tantalizing scent from the hallway, Buck bypassed the waiting room by sneaking in behind another patient and followed the softest, sweetest voice he'd ever heard.

"No, I cannot go easy on these cadets, Del. What the hell do you want me to do? Tell them it's okay to skim that mountain with the bottom of the plane? As long as you don't crash land or blow us up, we can fix the rest?"

It was her. His mate. She was close. Really close.

"Oh, I know." There was a sharp snap of fingers followed by a loud single clap. "The doofuses that can't fold their socks, let alone pack a chute. You know the ones, they always had momma to do everything for them. Doesn't matter if they have wings or not. They think I'm gonna be a stand in for their dear old mum."

Slapping his hand over his mouth to keep from laughing out loud as she put on a posh British accent, pronouncing mom as *mum*, Buck wanted to see her more than he wanted his next breath. Not only did his mate smell absolutely edible but she was also sassy and full of life. He already liked her...*a lot*. And so did the raging hard-on in his camos.

Creeping forward, he kept watching, moving ever closer as the conversation he was eavesdropping on just kept rolling along.

"Yeah, I get that," a second female voice, the one he knew went with the name Del and also happened to be carrying a shit-ton of irritation in it that was directed at his mate, retorted. "Nobody knows your process better than I do. This is the *second cadet* you've carried in here *today*."

"They're alive, aren't they?"

"Well, yes, but..."

"I've never had one die on my watch, have I?"

"Well, no, but—"

"No, but..." Chuckling, the sound full, robust, absolutely fantastic, his mate went on. "Is that your professional opinion, Dr. Weathersbee? Can I get a second? Don't you have like nineteen specialties?"

"I could ask you the same thing, Dr. Lightfoot." The doc's voice was filled with friendly admiration and a lot of affection. "Don't you have something like seven Ph.D.s and an M.D. but chose to jump out of completely good airplanes? And what's worse, teach others, who do not have the benefit of wings like yourself, to do the same?"

"I do!" Dr. Lightfoot—Buck's mate—laughed right out loud, that sound even a hundred times more intoxicating than her chuckle.

Heart racing, his palms suddenly sweaty, and his cock asking *"What the fuck, man? Can you hurry it up?"* Buck damned near hit the floor when she admitted with a serious case of the giggles, "I actually have ten, well, eleven if count the M.D., but they're all in stupid shit that keeps me inside and my eyes glued to a microscope. I need the feel of the wind through my wings..."

"And the sound of your own voice barking orders." Dr. Weathersbee laughed before dropping her voice several octaves. "Freddie, you can't toss cadets out of airplanes without their consent ever again. Is that understood?"

"Ma'am, yes, ma'am," his mate barked right back before hooting with laughter. "But honestly, Del, I didn't throw either of them out of the plane. They literally jumped out of their own accord, pulled the ripcord perfectly, then ran right into the same damned tree." Stopping to gasp and wheeze—even those sounds turning Buck on as he imagined her doing them naked and in his bed—his mate laughed, "It was like George of the Jungle in fatigues."

Needing to see her, to lay eyes on the one woman in all the world made just for him, Buck forgot to take another look around before he inched forward. Hand on the doorframe, eyes just about to get their first look at his mate, the honey badger's ears nearly fell off his head as a roar sounded from over his shoulder.

"What do you think you're doing, Cadet?"

Head slamming into said doorframe, Buck didn't even get to enjoy the stars dancing before his eyes. It all happened so fast.

A clawed hand clamped down on his shoulder, saving him from hitting the floor headfirst. Then before he knew what was happening, the entire world had gone on a spin cycle. "What do you have to say for yourself? Skulking around, listening to conversations that do not concern you. Speak now before I call Ms. Cooper and have you tossed out on your ear." The voice that had startled him, as well as the clawed hands that had grasped him, belonged to the biggest, angriest crow shifter he'd ever seen, who was dressed in FUCN'A nurse's scrubs.

"Well, I was… It's just that…"

"Looks like he's been in the wars, Hetty." Dr. Weathersbee chuckled from just over his other shoulder.

Pointing at the doctor, Buck attempted to keep the stammer out of his voice as he quickly explained, "Yeah, what she said, nurse"—eyes flashing to her gold name badge then right back to her narrowed, angry black eyes —"Thomas." Chuckling, an attempt to ease the tension and defuse the situation that failed miserably, Buck searched his mind for all the things he'd said to his mother to get out of all the similar situations that had come before. Sadly, Nurse Thomas was *not* the only authority figure to want to beat the fur right off his ass. The honey badger had more than ample references who could quote, chapter and verse, his many misdeeds and fuckups.

"I was sent here after an accident in Advanced Explosives. Professor—"

Not bothering to let him finish, her eyes already rolling as she pushed him toward a patient room, Nurse Thomas growled, "That damned dragon. When will he ever learn? These cadets are not ready for this shit. One day…"

"It's okay, Hetty," Dr. Weathersbee pacified. "I'm sure Professor Firestone does what he thinks is best for his students, just like you and I do. Let me finish with Dr. Lightfoot while you get Mr…umm…" Eyes flying back to his, the doctor shrugged. "What's your name, Cadet?"

"Blackthorne. Buck Blackthorne."

Then right back to the crow without missing a beat, she added, "…Mr. Blackthorne cleaned up and get his chart started."

"Yes, ma'am, Dr. Weathersbee."

And that was where it had ended. He didn't get to see his mate. Didn't even hear her voice one last time.

For the next four days, Buck had tried to get a look at the illustrious and incredibly elusive Dr. Lightfoot. Unfortunately, right after she visited the infirmary, Freddie—at least he knew her name—had left the Academy on some special mission.

Not even Olivia Owlgenthorpe, the second-year cadet with a specialty in computer hacking and a minor in web-based applications, had been able to get him *any* information on Freddie Lightfoot's whereabouts. So, when the weekend came, and he could go home for a couple of days, Buck jumped at the chance.

Tuning back into the running conversation between

his family members, Buck was just about to give his vote for steaks on the grill and corn on the cob for dinner when Shauna asked, "So, you gonna tell us who she is?"

"Or do we have to come up to that fancy school and find out for ourselves?" Jack inquired.

To which Spencer demanded, "And don't try to tell us that you haven't found your mate, 'cause we all just said the words Mom's strawberry pie with homemade vanilla ice cream and you didn't so much as blink an eye."

"Well, fuck," Buck groaned, running his fingers through his hair. "There are times I seriously hate each and every one of y'all."

Crinkling her nose and blowing him a kiss, Shauna teased, "Aww, I'd be hurt if I thought you were serious." Picking up the rag off the bar and throwing it right at his head, she ordered with a wink, "Now dish. I wanna know all about my future sister-in-law."

2

Flying over the tallest peak of the Serra da Mantiqueira just outside São Paulo, Brazil, for what felt like the hundredth time, Freddie cursed Kloe, her mission director in the Furry United Coalition. "What the literal fuck?" she spat to her empty plane.

"Why do I have to be the only available FUC agent who flies a plane that has ten Ph.D.s? Why do I have to be in nerdy, brainy crap like toxicology, physics, microbiology, and a lotta crap that doesn't go together but I wanted to learn? Oh, and why did I think it would be cool to learn ten languages, including Portuguese and Vietnamese, *arrrrrgggggh*, whatever! Why wasn't I born without a brain?!"

She paused her monologue with a frustrated growl, the leading doctor in the field of more things than she wanted to think about beat the yoke of her Lightfoot FUC jet with both hands. "Never do what your mom and dad tell you to do, kids. Do what *you* want. If you want to fly planes, do it! If you want to be a paratrooper and jump *out of* perfectly good planes, do it! If you want to be a scientist, well, fuck, do that, too. But make damned sure it's what *you* want. 'Cause let me tell you…"

Ending her rant with a huff and more guilt than she wanted to think about for dissing her parents, Freddie, aka Dr. Winifred F. Lightfoot, sighed. "Sorry, Moms. Sorry, Pops. You know what a shithead I can be when I'm having a rant.

"And it's not really them you're mad at," she mumbled.

She'd wanted to stay at the Academy. Wanted to go see her old friend, Matt Firestone. Wanted to get a good, hard look at the honey badger who made her heart go pitter-pat and her inner minx scream, "Come home to momma, big boy!"

But she'd had no choice but to follow FUC orders and fly off to investigate the nutjob in the middle of Fucking Nowhere, Brazil, who was destroying every last coffee bean and the fields where they're grown.

Freddie focused on what had to be done instead of what she couldn't change. *So, if our intel is right, this idiot—whoever they may be—thinks they can corner the coffee market by hijacking shipments and killing the crops.*

Shaking her head, running the fingers of her gloved hand through her long black curls, the winged tree frog shifter shook her head. "Why are people so stupid? Coffee? Really? Talk about cutting off the lifeblood of the world. Thank the Goddess I have three cases hidden in the back of the pantry at home."

Hand to her forehead, she blew out an exasperated breath with such vigor that it ended in a raspberry. "I gotta fix this shit before I run out. Freddie Lightfoot without caffeine is not a Freddie Lightfoot anyone wants to meet." *Especially not her one and only mate.*

Shaking her head, she added with a grumble, "Come to think of it, there's not one damned person in the whole world I want to meet before they've had their morning cup o' joe or I've had mine."

Laughing out loud, her mood lifted at the thought of her dear old dad, the King of the Royal Blue Butterfly Frolic and the man who'd poured Freddie her first cup of steaming hot java. *Freddie, my girl, you can't fix stupid with duct tape. Try coffee. If that doesn't work, there's always the blow torch.*

"Damn, Dad, I miss you like crazy." Refusing to think about the loss of her parents, or anything else sad for that matter, she returned to reciting the chemicals used by the latest Most Wanted Dickhead on the FUC's list.

"Okay, I get everything on the list, but why the hell did the techs find wolfsbane in the soil samples? That shit doesn't grow in Brazil, and it's not worth diddly-squat to anybody except florists to make an arrangement pretty and purple." Needing more clarification, she hit the button on her plane's yoke, the one decorated with a picture of a phone receiver. Directing Fifi, the automated attendant she named after her first puppy, a coal-black, two-hundred-pound Great Dane, she deadpanned, "Fifi, call Delilah."

"As you wish, Freddie," the high, Scooby-Doo-sounding automated voice responded.

Listening to the annoying ring of the phone, she was just about to hang up when her best friend, the resident doctor at FUCN'A and one of the smartest women she'd ever known, Dr. Delilah F. Weathersbee answered, "Hey, Ace, how's tricks?"

"Holy shit." Freddie laughed out loud. "How much have you had to drink?"

"Not even a drop," Del slurred. "My new research assistant forgot to turn off the valve on the nitrous oxide and we're all recovering from a serious case of the giggles."

"Dammit." Freddie chuckled her curse, smiling from ear-to-ear. "You have all the fun when *I'm* not there. Something about that isn't fair. *Puhlease* tell me somebody videoed that shit."

"Oh, yeah." Del giggled, the effects of the gas still quite evident in the usually calm, collected, and always politically correct physician. "I'm not sure it'll be in focus and not of the floor, but everybody had their phones out."

"Even you?"

"No," the doctor scoffed. "You know I never know where that damned thing is." Voice trailing off, Freddie had her suspicions that the dragonfly shifter had taken so long to answer because she hadn't been able to find her phone right away.

"Okay, Del, I'm gonna let you go." She snickered, knowing she wasn't going to get any answers from Delilah until her friend was sober.

"No, no, no, no, no." The doctor made it into a song ending with a giggled "No-no-nonononono - noooo" to the tune of The Kink's song, "Lola."

Not wanting to be rude, Freddie suggested, "How about I let you go for *now?* You can call me back when you're feeling more like yourself."

"But—but, but… But…"

There was a long pause. Freddie could hear the shuffling of papers, the whir and the slam of a drawer being quickly opened and shut before Delilah chuckled. "I just love you so much, Freddie. You're my best friend. I don't know what I would do without you. What am I gonna do without you?" Her voice went from mushy to concerned in the blink of an eye. "What am I…"

"Del. Del. Delilah!" Freddie ended up yelling, hurrying on when the doctor finally stopped speaking.

"I don't want us to hang up."

"I know, honey, but I need to let you go."

"You do? Oh, yeah, that's right. Bye, Freddie."

And with that, the phone went dead.

Blowing out a long breath, Freddie sighed and hit Fifi's button one more time. "Call Miranda."

Two seconds later and half a ring, the always cheerful, bouncy voice of her FUC buddy and saber-toothed bunny shifter, Mirada Brownsmith, bubbled through Freddie's jet. "Hey, chica. What's up?"

"Hey! I have a favor to ask."

"Shoot."

"Are you anywhere near the Academy?"

"Nope. Why?" Miranda quickly answered, sounding a little distracted.

"I needed somebody to check on Del. Her research assistant gassed the whole clinic with nitrous oxide, and well, let's just say, it's worse than Susan St. Bernard's bachelorette party last year."

"Oh, damn." Miranda snickered, quickly adding, "Hang on just a sec."

Listening to the rushed murmuring of one of the best and smartest and caring people Freddie had ever met, she was ready to tell the bunny that she'd let her go when Miranda came back. "Sorry about that. We just finished a case out here in the middle of the swamp somewhere, and I had to call it in."

"Oh, damn, I'll let you go. Sorry…"

"Oh, hush," Miranda shushed with a giggle. "I always have time for you. Let me call Matt. I know he's still at FUCN'A. He can run up and check on Delilah for us."

"Well, hell, I should've thought of that."

"No way, chica, then I couldn't have been the super-hero of this tale." Laughing out the loud, the sound always making Freddie feel better, the bunny added, "Now, I do have to let you go. Sorry, but my bear is testy. It's been at least three hours since he had anything to eat. Be safe and call me when you get back."

"How did you…"

But Miranda had already hung up. Muttering to herself for the umpteenth time, *how did she… son of a buckethead!* She'd heard the sound of the engines. Bopping herself in the forehead with the heel of her hand, she snickered. "Note to self, create nonflammable insulation to silence the rumble inside the cabin of a jet. Rule number whatever—never let anyone know what you're doing till you want them to know. Where is my brain today?"

On the impending shortage of your dear sweet coffee and thoughts of that sexy-ass honey badger…

"Yeah, yeah, yeah." She answered her own wayward

thoughts. "I seriously do not have time for this lovey-dovey crap right now."

But you want it...

"Oh, shut up," she growled, shutting off that side of her brain, switching to her analytic side, which everyone called her super-computer because of its ability for total recall. Freddie named it her "little grey cells," quoting the famous Belgian detective in her favorite old movies,

She brought to mind the list of substances found by the crime scene techs, and she kept coming back to the wolfsbane. "Okay, so if I were an evil genius, or a dipshit looking to corner the market on the sweetest, dark liquid to ever be poured from a pot, why would I use wolfsbane?"

Tapping her bottom lip while she bit the inside of her cheek, she said, "Well, we know it's harmful to humans, shifters, anybody with a body chemistry close to *homo sapiens*, but all the antidotes are readily available. And even when it's a threat to shifters, there's a large percentage of us dual-natured hotties who aren't bothered by it all. Let's see..."

Her analysis was paused as she approached her destination and realized that a particularly weird-looking cloud was going to make her change course. Taking the jet left and making a wide circle, she flew over the burned-out coffee fields. Mile after mile of blackened stalks and soot-covered soil. It made her heart hurt not only for the coffee but also for the environment and all the living creatures she knew had perished.

"I'll avenge y'all, my friends. I promise." Inhaling deeply, the fresh scent of coffee filling her senses, she was forced to groan. "That's just not fair. Something this horrible should not smell this good."

Turning her attention back to the burned fields, she used her enhanced vision and the binoculars built into the lenses of her sunglasses. They were the coolest things ever. Something she and Willem had worked to perfect, the glassnoculars were only to be used by FUC Agents and were the godsend she'd intended for just such a mission.

Making another, tighter circle, she dropped closer to the treetops on the perimeter of the fields. Just about to give up and land anyway, a flash in her peripheral vision had Freddie jerking the yoke to the right and pulling back as hard and fast as she could.

Climbing higher and higher, listening for gunfire, a rocket launcher, hell, even a peashooter with good range, Freddie leveled off and banked left. Decelerating ever so slightly, she zeroed in on the exact spot of the flash.

Tapping the arm of her glasses, increasing the magnification on her glassnoculars, it took less than a heartbeat to locate the source of the flare. "Debris," she hissed. "Glass and metal. Probably wood, too. Gotta check this shit out. Seems stupid, but so does everything else about this case."

Heading straight for the most massive outcropping atop the smallest mountain in range, Freddie expertly landed her plane. Jumping out of the cockpit while the propeller was still spinning, she shoved her arms into the straps of her multi-colored camouflage backpack, giving it a wiggle to be sure it was in just the right spot.

Walking to the edge of the outcropping, Freddie called

to the being with whom she shared her soul, the winged tree frog and princess with major 'tude, who she'd nick-named Rainbow Bright because Raeanna Bree sounded way too formal and stuffy. It also helped that her wings were nothing short of a gorgeous kaleidoscope of the best colors when unfurled. *"Hey, Bright, how about we take a spin? Check out what smells so good?"*

"Oh, now you need me, do you?" came the winged tree frog's sassy reply. *"That stupid machine was good enough for you an hour ago. You said you didn't want to tire me out. Said you didn't—"*

"Okay, smartass," Freddie huffed. *"I wanted to get here as quickly as possible, and you tend to, well, that is to say, oh fuck it, you dawdle, Bright. You want to stop and smell every damned flower, taste every dewdrop, look at—"*

"So, because I appreciate the beauty in the world, of life, of every living thing created by the Great Goddess Herself, I get left up here in the dark all the time? Is that what you're saying, Winifred?"

"Don't. Call. Me. Winifred," Freddie replied through gritted teeth, trying really hard not to snarl and failing miserably. *"And I did not leave you trapped up there in the dark. You can see everything I see, every day, all the time, without fail. Stop with the drama queen act."*

"I am not being a drama queen, I am a drama princess, because we are, in fact, the Princess of the Royal Blue Butterfly Frolic. We have been blessed by the Goddess. We are—"

"Special little snowflakes," Freddie scoffed with a very adamant roll of her eyes, which she was sure to turn inward so that her alter ego couldn't miss it. *"Yeah, yeah, yeah, I know all about us. Now, can you—"*

"*And about this thing with the honey badger. When exactly are you going to introduce yourself? Don't you think you should at least get to know him before he expects you to start popping out little rainbow-striped furbabies with wings?*"

"*Well, fuck, I hadn't thought about that,*" Freddie groused, instantly changing her tone and sighing wistfully. "*I was just fantasizing about those big, strong arms wrapped around me, holding me close while we stare into each other's eyes. And what the muscles in that super-fine ass will feel like when I get my hands on them. And if he knows how to kiss me till my thighs go up in flames... Do you think he knows how to kiss like the big, strong, burly, sex god he looks to be, Bright?*" Fanning herself, suddenly way more turned on than a woman without a man by her side should ever be, Freddie blew out a long breath, letting the words ride her exhale. "*Please, dear Goddess, tell me he knows how to kiss. Can you even remember the last time we were kissed by a man?*"

"No, I cannot," Bright snapped way too matter-of-factly. "*And I don't think that's what's most important. First of all, you need him to understand who you are, that you are not cold-blooded, and that he is your mate, ordained by the Goddess and the Universe and the only man you are meant to ever be with... forever.*"

"*Damn, girl, you are a serious buzz kill.*"

"No, I most assuredly am not," her alter ego snapped. "*I am a realist and here to keep you from leaping before you look and getting our collective asses in a sling we cannot get out of. And you know as well as I do that he is the first son of Janice Blackthorne, the Leader of the renowned Blackthorne Honey Badger Clan. We both read the file. And, as such, she, Janice Blackthorne, will forbid your mating to her son if she thinks*" *you are cold-blooded, as your heritage initially suggests. She wants a gaggle of little Blackthornes running all over the countryside. It's the way of the furry shifters. There is no denying that. The call to procreate cannot be denied."*

"Well, shit, I hadn't thought about that."

"I am aware." Bright heavily sighed. *"I am sure you remember, but it bears repeating that, for a large part of the time, pretty much always and forever, we share a brain."*

"Yeah, the highlight of my life."

"And your sarcasm fills me with all the happy tingles, too."

"No, you're right. I'll deal with my love life when we get back," Freddie snapped in return, pulling herself together and shoving all thoughts of one very sexy, panty-melting honey badger to the back of her mind. *"Now, hop to it, Princess Raeanna Bree. I bow to your excellence in flight and promise to keep my mouth shut until we are safely at the bottom of this mountain. Also, take a whiff once you're out here. The scent of sweet, sweet java is magnificent. Just don't think about why it's here or the black smoke polluting the air."*

"Guess that'll have to do."

"You betcha. 'Cause that's all you're gettin', hot stuff."

Giving the reins of her body and soul to her alter ego —the human-size frog with wings—and making sure her backpack was still secure, Freddie went back to working on the puzzle of the wolfsbane. The herbicide *diquat* made perfect sense. It killed everything it touched above ground—leaves, buds, the precious little coffee beans themselves. Glyphosate was a systemic herbicide. It would've killed the roots of those little beauties in less than twenty-four hours. Then there was pentachlorophenol that the lead scientist of the ICS—

Investigation of the Crime Scene—Enzo, a really book-smart aardvark shifter who needed more practical experience, in her humble opinion, had told the boss didn't make sense.

Yes, it does, dear Enzo, Freddie thought. *Because the two herbicides together give the stupid dipshit trying to take away one of my top three reasons for living, my coffee, a ninety-nine-point-nine percent chance of killing every one of those precious little white-flowered, red-beaned, life-giving plants in one fell swoop. Can you say asshole? I know I can.*

Growling the last part, she finished her thought. *Then to be sure he'd murdered them all, the shit-for-brains bad guy of my very own horror story made the easiest, cheapest, and from the amounts on that report,- biggest homemade bomb. Using fertilizer, gunpowder, and hydrogen peroxide finished off any of the leafed lovelies who fought hard to survive and, in its wake, left the ground unfertile for... for...*

Quickly calculating the amounts she'd seen in the report, she shouted in her mind, *"Ten years? What the heck and hootenannies? Hurry up, Bright. We gotta figure this shit out, like yesterday. Just let me get my hands on the little SOB."*

"How do you know he's little?" Rainbow Bright offhandedly asked.

"Because they all are. If not in reality, in all the ways that matter."

Bringing them in for a landing as smooth as creamy peanut butter on hot toast, Rainbow Bright happily chirped, *"Your turn now,"* before receding to the back of Freddie's mind with a, *"and you were right. The scent of roasting coffee is only tainted by the act of terrorism that caused it."*

Freddie returned to her human form and replied, *"My thoughts exactly."*

Shifting for the woman and her winged tree frog had always been precisely that seamless. Even from the first time, there'd been no pain, no dysphoria, nothing more than moving from the front to the rear and then back again in her soul. Freddie really felt sorry for the big, brawny shifters who'd told her how painful their change could be.

"Wonder if it hurts when Buck shifts into his honey badger?"

"Well, I wouldn't know," Bright sassed. *"Because you didn't talk to him before setting off on this foolhardy mission."*

"Foolhardy? Exactly how is finding the asshole depriving the world—and me—of the greatest drink in the history of all history foolhardy? Tell me, Bright. Tell me now. Do you really want to be stuck with me for the rest of forever without the aid of caffeine in its most splendid form?"

Sucking in a deep breath, she added before her alter ego could respond, *"And if that's not enough, he's a murderer of at least three humans and of more little critters than we can ever ascertain the number of."*

"I am not saying that, and you know it. I am simply voicing my opinion. Of course, all of that matters way more than your coffee consumption. I've been telling you to make the switch to green tea for a month of Sundays."

"And I've been telling you to get stuffed."

Completely ignoring that Freddie had even spoken, the winged tree frog kept going. *"I think that coming out here alone, with no backup, in the back-ass of Nowhere, Brazil, in the middle of a valley surrounded by a mountain range where there is absolutely no cell reception was not your smartest move. And you, my dearest Freddie, are no dummy."*

"Did I have a choice?"

"You always have a choice, Freddie."

"Yeah, well, up yours, too."

Slamming her mental blocks into place and securing them with the enchantment she'd inherited from her mother's side of the family, the magic of the great witch and Celtic goddess, Cerridwen, Freddie gave a sassy retort of her own. *"Now, just sit there and think about that, Miss Raeanna Bree, princess of my big round booty."*

Shaking off her irritation and shoving aside the guilt she felt over putting Bright in time-out, Freddie dressed quickly, then opened her mind as far as it would go. Letting her eyes slide shut, she blocked the images of the one and only incredibly sexy honey badger, in the buff, spread out on her bed, waiting for her to join him, and focused on finding the exact location of the fire.

"Thank the Goddess that I got a decent sense of smell from both Mom and Dad. Sure, I sometimes wish Pops would've been a wolf or a bear. Hell, I'd have taken chimp, anything with a few more muscles. It would've... Whoa, looky right there, folks. Got it on the first try. Give me a cookie. Preferably chocolate chip and dipped in coffee."

Yep, gotta get this crisis under control. My brain is not firing on all cylinders.

With her mind's eye locking on the smoldering rubble of what she immediately recognized as a rather large ranch-style *hacienda*, Freddie opened her real eyes—the two just above her nose—and with the map in her head, marched forward. Almost immediately entrenched in a dense forest of kapok-bearing ceiba trees enlaced with vines and creepers, she pulled out her machete. Designed by Willem, an Amur leopard shifter, the head of the FUCN'A Design and Development Division and one of her good friends, the machete went on every mission with her, even those in the middle of the city. However, she hadn't gotten to try the leopard's newest modification.

Swinging the long sharp blade like it was a bat, she was Babe Ruth, and it was game seven of the 1932 World Series. From one slash to the next, a loud whir emanated from the leather-covered handle, and the machete started to vibrate in her hand. Stopping midstride and midstroke, Freddie felt her eyes open as wide as they would go when long, sharp spikes appeared, covering all the edges of the blade, and began to spin like a buzz saw.

"Son of a biscuit eater!" she cheered. "Way to freakin' go, Willem. You are the rock star of all rock stars. I'm gonna kiss you square on the lips the next time I see you."

Pushing through the rest of the thick foliage between her and the smoldering rubble, careful not to damage anything the creatures who called the woods home would need, Freddie stopped fifty yards after emerging from the dense foliage. Sliding her thumb up the inside of the handle, she happily mumbled, "And that's another reason why you're my brother from another mother, dear Willem. The simplicity of your designs does my heart good. Make the off switch the opposite of the on switch. Perfection."

Stowing the machete back in her pack before digging out a bottle of water, Freddie used the guise of getting something to drink to engage her fantastic echolocation and keen sense of hearing. Although there weren't as many sounds as she was sure there'd been the day before, she quickly picked out the scritch of a sloth's long nails scratching across tree branches and the capybaras in their caves at least five miles behind her.

"I see you looking at me through the leaves of that fern, little monkey," she whispered, smiling when the tiny guy's eyes opened even wider before he turned to scamper off.

Tired of talking to herself and her conscience working overtime to make her feel like a real horse's ass, Freddie opened her mental shields and beamed, *"Hey, Bright!"*

When no reply came, but she could see the winged tree frog pouting in the deepest corner of her mind, Freddie gave up and went straight to the apology portion of their scheduled programming. *"I'm sorry, Bright. Really sorry. That was a dick move. Just 'cause I didn't like what you were saying doesn't mean I get to play the Wicked Witch of the West and lock you in the dungeon."*

Watching as Rainbow Bright's head turned to the side, the beautiful shine of her emerald green and red-rimmed eyes slowly returning to their usual glowing luster, Freddie went in for the kill. *"How about, to make it up to you, when we get home, I let you take our cadets out on a hang-gliding exercise? We'll call it Professor Bright's Intro to Riding the Winds."*

Up on her tiny little webbed feet and doing pirouettes from one side of Freddie's mind to the other, Rainbow Bright sang, *"Oh, yes. Oh, yes. Oh, yes."* To the tune of Handel's "Hallelujah Chorus."

"Are you sure, Bright? I'd hate to have to twist your

wing." Freddie chuckled, a sense of relief washing over her that she and her alter ego were once again on good terms.

"Oh, Freddie, you are such a...WATCH OUT!"

And just like that, shit got really real.

3

"Come on, Buck," his mother cajoled, her voice carrying that *mom tone* that meant she was about three-point-three seconds from demanding he tell her everything. Even her hand was cocked at the ready to bop him in the back of his head.

Running his fingers through his hair for what seemed like the hundredth time, the honey badger took a deep breath and slowly let it out. Preparing to spill the beans, ready for the piles of shit his family would shovel—all in good fun—his prayers were answered. Just like that, he was saved.

The huge wooden double doors at the front of the bar swung open. The scent of grizzly bear and saber-toothed bunny filled the air. Head popping up, eyes opening as wide as they would go, he'd never been happier to see two people in his own long life.

"Look what the cat dragged in," Buck teased with loud laughter as he planted his hands on the bar and vaulted the scuffed wooden top in one easy move. Holding out his hand, the heels of his boots hitting the hardwood as he crossed the room, he greeted his friends with a cheery, "Long time, no see."

"Hell, yeah," Chase Brownsmith, the huge, usually grumpy and always direct grizzly bear, agreed. Grabbing Buck's hand, he added with a glare that had his bushy eyebrows completely covering his eyelids, "So long that you forgot my phone number."

"Huh?" Buck was momentarily confused.

Then it hit him like a ton of bricks, making him backpedal so fast his whole family started laughing and his brother Jack shouted, "Kick his ass, Chase."

"Oh, shit, no…" Shaking his head, trying to extract his hand from the unrelenting grip of the grizzly bear, he scrambled to explain to the old family friend. "It's not like that. It was a spur-of-the-moment decision. I mean ever since Shauna joined that other Agency, I'd been thinkin' about doin' somethin' besides sittin' around here and runnin' a bar."

Nervously scratching at the stubble covering his jaw as he wondered if Chase was ever going to let go of his hand, the honey badger's rambling explanation continued, getting faster with every word. "You know how it is. I missed the action. Wanted to be doing something that made a difference."

Snapping his head to the side and looking right at his mother and brothers, he winked. "Goddess knows, Mom, Jack, and Spence have got this place under control. They only put up with me 'cause they've got to."

Turning back to the couple only when his mom smiled and nodded, Buck looked to Miranda, Chase's wife, and a saber-toothed bunny shifter for support. "It all happened so fast. I made a call. Talked to a recruiter, and within two hours, they emailed me all the entrance stuff. Said that I was fast-tracked because of my extensive military background."

"Guess they needed somebody to blow shit up," Spencer heckled from the background. "Isn't that what you did, bro? Make bombs out of your own stock of ladies' panties?"

Ignoring his brother, Buck was happy to see Miranda nodding and smiling. His hopes took a serious upswing as she laid her hand atop her hubby's and snickered. "Chase, honey, I think you better give Buck back his hand."

"And don't be too pissed, big guy," Shauna chimed in, walking up beside Buck but talking to the grizzly. "The butthead didn't tell me either. I had to find out from Mom. So, y'all aren't the lone strangers. Dumbshit left us all out."

"Sure as hell didn't text me," Buck's brother-in-law added, appearing beside his mate and holding out his hand to Chase. "Abe Silverblade, good to meet ya."

"Oh, shit, sorry," Buck jumped in. "Where are my manners?"

"Lost, right along with my phone number," the grizzly grumbled before smiling and chuckling as he took Abe's hand. "Chase Brownsmith, and this is my wife, Miranda."

"Nice to meet y'all." Abe chatted away like he'd known the couple forever.

Something is up. I can feel it...

"We're about to cook up half a cow, a half-dozen

chickens, and pretty much all of a pig. Certified non-sentient, of course. Y'all wanna join us for dinner?"

"Hell, yeah, they wanna join us," Janice hollered from where she stood behind the bar. "The more, the merrier." Setting frosty bottles of beer in a line down the bar, the matriarch continued. "We've got all the meat you could want, Chase. I've even got two Alaskan salmon back in the cooler with your name on 'em."

"Sign me up, Janice," the grizzly said, grabbing a bottle of beer and drinking it down in one swallow.

Watching his mom head toward the kitchen, sure things were about to get back to normal, Buck held his breath when Janice stopped with both hands on the swinging gray door, her head turned to the side. Eyes shining with a whole lot of mischief, he was sure his momma was about to out him for having a mate, when thankfully she only yoo-hooed, "And, Chase, I have four fresh strawberry pies, a fresh batch of honey buns, and homemade ice cream for dessert."

"Janice, you have always been and always will be my favorite honey badger in the whole wide world."

Laughing as his mother disappeared into the kitchen, Buck finally let out the breath he'd been holding since Shauna said the word "sister-in-law" nearly ten minutes before. Grabbing a beer and tipping it back, he didn't get to enjoy even a drop as his sister crooned in the way only a little sister who's up to no good could. "Hey, Buck, time to fess up. You've made us wait long enough. Tell us all about your mate. I bet Chase and Miranda know her."

Spitting beer so far and with such force that it flew across the bar and splashed dead center on the huge antique mirror that had been his great-great-granddad's, Buck coughed and wheezed, sputtered and spat, barely getting out, "Wh-What th-the hell, Shauna?"

"Oh, hell no," Chase growled, a smile crossing his face from one side to the other. "Don't you go yellin' at your sister there, big guy." Poking Buck in the chest with the end of his meaty index finger, the big grizzly went in for the kill. "You've got a mate at FUCN'A and you didn't call me to get the details on her?"

"Well, umm… *no?*" Buck shrugged.

"What is wrong with you? I know your parents raised you better than that."

"Now, honey," Miranda intervened, "give Buck a break. Maybe he was just waiting for the right time." Looking at him with big bunny eyes open wide as she gave a tiny, jerky nod toward her hubby. "You know how it is when you find your mate. Everything kinda goes haywire and you—"

"Blow up the fucking explosives lab?" The words were out of Buck's mouth long before his muddled brain ever engaged.

"You what?" everyone in attendance blurted out in perfect unison, laughing like he was Red Fucking Skelton.

"You?" Jack guffawed so loud he had tears running down his face. "Please, dear Goddess, tell me that you were building a bomb with ladies' panties again and this time you ended up with them on your head."

"No," Buck groaned, pissed at himself for being a total nincompoop and especially for answering his brother's stupid question.

Inhaling deeply, his already broad chest expanding to

full capacity, Chase got his laughter just barely under control. Watching the grizzly try to act like he wasn't enjoying Buck's embarrassment would've been funny, if the honey badger hadn't been the butt of his own joke. Instead, he could only stand there and groan as Chase asked, "So, did the little woman see you try to blow yourself up?"

"No."

"Does she know it happened?"

"Yes."

"So, she's another cadet?"

"No."

"Wait!" Miranda stepped between Buck and her hubby's back-and-forth. "Is she a teacher or a staff member?"

"What's the difference?"

"Oh my Goddess," Janice squawked, reentering the front of the bar just in time to chastise her eldest son. "Did you seriously eat the academy handbook? How have you lived this long? I worry about my grandchildren."

"I know the difference." He sighed. "I just…" Hand back in his hair, he groaned, "I need another beer. Hell, make it a shot of Jack."

Taking the clear highball glass containing two fingers of his favorite amber drink, Buck downed it in one gulp. Taking a second to enjoy the fiery burn, he mumbled, "It's Freddie Lightfoot."

Hoping everyone was still too busy discussing his inability to discern between a teacher and a regular staff member, which wasn't what he'd meant but would never get the opportunity to correct.

As if I didn't know. Good Goddess, can a guy get a break? I'm telling the toughest crowd in my entire world the name of my mate. Can I get a little love? Damn, I hope Chase and Miranda don't know her. Please, please, please...

But of course they knew her, and so did his big dragon brother-in-law.

"No, shit?" Abe bellowed, smiling with way more teeth than Buck was completely comfortable with. "Met her at a DPA..." Glancing at Chase and Miranda, he explained, "Dragon Protection Agency meeting." Then back to every-one, he continued. "Matt Firestone brought her to talk to Gil, my boss, about some aerosol solvent she's working on. It encases a bomb so it can be moved to a safe place to be defused, or maybe, it was that it paralyzes people so we can apprehend them with less chance of a fight and inno-cents getting hurt. Hell, it was something."

"You're really into the technical shit, huh?" Buck snorted.

"Don't sass your elders," Shauna snapped, swatting his arm. "My honey knows a lot of stuff. Don't you worry about that." Not even taking a breath, his baby sister switched gears, the twinkle in her eye turning devious. "So, how did you meet? When are you bringing her home to meet everybody? Where's the wedding? Do I get to be a bridesmaid? Are you—"

"Hold it!" Buck roared, giving a single sharp clap of his hands, which echoed throughout the suddenly silent Sundowner.

Taking a deep breath and looking around the room as he exhaled, the honey badger nodded to Abe then to Chase before beginning. "Since you will not let up until I am completely and totally humiliated, I will tell you that there was no permanent damage to the explosives lab, or to me. Thank you very much for asking. *Sheesh!* With friends and family like y'all, I'm safer facing all Kole's goons and Mastermind's and Mother Jones' at the same time with one arm tied behind my back and my honey badger taking the day off."

Thank goodness I'm up to date on the recent villains FUC's faced. At least I sound like I know what I'm talkin' about. "Baffle 'em with bullshit, Buck, my boy," Dad used to say.

Not letting anyone talk and working hard not to burst out laughing at the shocked looks on everybody's faces, he went right on ahead and told them the whole story. Not bothering to leave out the part where he ran his head into the wall. Winding up, he chuckled. "And I shit you not, Nurse Thomas threatened to take my temperature rectally."

Holding his hands up shoulder-width apart, he went on. "With a thermometer I know they use on elephants. She then added that she would lock me in a room with the Rat Sisters—twin cadets who truly personify everything about their alter egos— if I ever showed up in the clinic with pieces of aluminum can in my 'manly bits' again."

He made exaggerated air quotes with both hands to be sure they understood that was *precisely* what the crow shifter had said before ending with a perfect imitation of the nurse. "And take a shower. You smell like a brewery.'"

"That's old Hetty for you." Miranda chuckled. "She's something else. Best drill sergeant the Academy could have. Awesome nurse, too. Shitty bedside manner. But she really is one in a million."

"You're tellin' me." Buck guffawed. "She scared the shit right outta me."

For a few seconds, the honey badger thought he might actually be off the hook. That because he'd been honest and told them the whole mortifying story, his family and friends might just let it all go and enjoy the evening. But he was wrong...dead wrong.

It took less than a minute before Shauna was up on her feet, marching back toward him and asking, "So, why didn't you go find this Dr. Lightfoot? Sweep her off her feet with that Buck Blackthorne charm?"

Pinching his cheek, she gave him a slobbery kiss on the exact same spot. "Don't tell me when faced with the one woman in all the world made for him that my big brother, the roughest, toughest, sweet-talkin'-est honey badger ever born"—she lifted her arms and flexed her biceps and kissed the right one just like he used to do in his much younger, much stupider days— "choked."

Making the loudest, most horrible gagging and coughing sounds, his little sister, Goddess bless her heart, kept right on ragging on him like it was her birthday and he was the piñata. "Did you *cough* choke *gag-choke* big bro? *ahem*?"

Arm slung over her tummy as she fought a serious case of the giggles that refused to be stifled, Shauna leaned into her mate and burst out with, "Did you lose your nerve? Did that cute little smarty-pants get ya'll tangled up in your underwear? The white cotton BVDs, not the pink silk ones you use for bombmaking?"

Shaking his head and rolling his eyes, Buck downed what was left of his beer as everybody took a turn picking on him. He knew it was all in good fun. Hell, he would've done the same to any one of them had the boot been on the other paw.

Finally, as things died down, he answered his sister's last question. "For your information, Mrs. Shauna Silverblade, I did go back to talk to her, the next day, after I was all healed and did not in the slightest resemble the walking dead. I even looked her up, found out her sched-ule, and went to see her when I knew she'd be alone, but she wasn't there."

"According to my friend with the magic fingers"—wiggling his own digits in the air and waggling his eyebrows, Buck chuckled—"who could hack the Pentagon if we needed her to, Dr. Freddie Lightfoot is on a mission in Brazil."

"The coffee field burnings." Miranda asked, her eyes shooting to Chase's as her ever-ready smile turned to a frown.

"Yeah, that's what the classified file said."

"Son…" Chase scolded with that single word as he shook his head. "You're gonna get your ass kicked out before you barely get started. Hacking classified FUC files? What were you thinkin'?"

"He had a good reason." Miranda jumped to Buck's defense, for which he would forever be grateful. "This is love, and Freddie is his mate. He needed to know where she was." Bopping the end of the grizzly's nose with the tip of her finger, the bunny added, "You would've done the same thing if I'd have gone MIA."

"Yeah, okay," Chase conceded before pointing his finger at Buck and ordering, "But she's not MIA. We know where she is, right?" With another heavy sigh, he reprimanded, "But I get it. Just don't do that shit again. You get caught and not even I can save your ass."

"But he would try." Miranda nodded emphatically as she pulled her phone from her back pocket and swiped her thumb across the screen. "Freddie called me just a little while ago."

The little hairs on the back of Buck's neck stood on end at precisely the same second his inner beast snarled, *"What the hell? Why are we just hearing about this now? Didn't you tell them like five minutes ago that Freddie was our mate?"*

"Chill, Harry. Let the woman talk."

Hanging on the bunny's every word, sweat trickling down his back and his right foot tapping a steady tempo on the rung of his barstool, Buck didn't even breathe. He only asked, "And?"

"Oh, yeah," Miranda chirped, lifting the phone to her ear. "I was handing off a detainee and had to go. She said we'd talk later."

Tuning in to the ringing of the phone, Buck counted the seconds. Praying to hear Freddie answer with some snappy reply, Buck's fist closed so tightly on the empty bottle in his grasp that amber shards of glass flew in every direction when her voicemail happily replied, "You've reached Freddie Lightfoot. You know what to do."

4

No sooner had Rainbow Bright screamed her warning than Freddie was forcing their shift with a flash of magic that had her head spinning and the bagel she ate right before takeoff threatening to make an all-too-real reappearance. Snatching the control of the five-foot-eleven-inch winged tree frog from Freddie, Bright flapped her wings like she had suddenly become an angel, it was Judgment Day, and St. Peter was ringing the golden bell while hollering, "Last call."

Cutting through the air stream better than anything Boeing ever made, Bright's magic popped and crackled all around them. She was leaving the jet stream of all jet streams in her wake, burning the rubber of the sky. Whatever she'd seen had put the fear of the goddess in her beautiful butterfly booty, and the princess wasn't wasting any time getting them both the heck out of Dodge.

Looking one way and then the other, using Rainbow Bright's eyes like they were *glassnoculars*, Freddie screamed, *"What the fuck? What is happeni—"* Gasping when her eyes finally found the what, the why, and most definitely the who, her tone changed from mildly worried to completely freaked out and was heading at a high rate of speed toward a nervous breakdown.

Going up an octave and getting louder by at least ten decibels from one syllable to the next, Freddie screamed, *"Shut the front frikkin' door. What the fudge nuggets am I lookin' at? And when the schnickey doodles did I forget how to cuss?"*

She couldn't believe her eyes. It was something out of her worst nightmares and, actually, a couple of her daydreams while getting her doctorate in prehistoric lifeforms.

"I have no clue," Bright panted, her enormous rainbow-striped wings working triple time. *"Did you make this crap happen? Will it into existence? Let the hocus pocus you got from your momma get loose without supervision? Didn't you—"*

"Yes, I did," Freddie snapped before becoming so befuddled she sounded like one of her first-year astrophysics students. *"But I didn't... I couldn't... It can't be... Can it?"*

The silence spoke volumes. If she couldn't answer her own questions and Rainbow Bright was coming up empty-handed, one of two things was going on—(A) They'd accidentally opened a portal to an alternate dimension, or (B) The whole coffee bean caper was a ruse.

She was going with B.

Having studied on every continent in the world, some more than four times, and having cataloged lifeforms that modern science said did not exist, Freddie freely admitted, *"I've never seen anything like it. Have you?"*

"Would you be pissed if I said, Duh?" came Bright's

sarcastic reply. *"Since we share a brain and eyes and experiences and—"*

"Yeah, yeah, yeah, I get it, smartass." Freddie sighed. *"What I am asking is, in your other lifetimes, or whatever it is you call the time you've spent with the other, umm... well, shit... the..."*

"Other half of my soul. I only had one of those that wasn't you. It was your great-grandmother. She was killed way too early, and I was given another chance by the Great Goddess. We've had this conversation more times than I care to remember."

"Well, forgive me for forgetting. I am looking at a dozen.... No. Wait..." Muttering to herself, *"Thirteen, fourteen, fifteen..."* Then right back to Bright, she rushed on. *"Fifteen. Yes, that's a ten plus five for those of you who chose to be mean to me in a time of crisis—ahem, Bright—let's call them, well, fuck, I don't know what to call them. How about lifeforms?"*

"You're more eloquent than me," Bright grumbled, a compliment that didn't come very often. *"I was thinking fucked-up fuckers from Fucksville."*

"Bright!" Freddie gasped, biting the inside of her cheek to keep from laughing out loud. *"What were you just telling me about cursing? Something about it lowering my IQ, as well as yours."*

"Oh, shut up." Landing on the same outcropping they'd taken off from not ten minutes before, Rainbow Bright clipped, *"Time to switch back, sweetcheeks. That trip took all the jet fuel I had and then some. Goddess, give me a shot of tequila and a stage full of naked men. Momma needs a recharge."*

"No worries." Freddie readily agreed. *"Thanks for saving my ass. Oh, and I thought we were staying outta strip clubs since you high-jacked my body and spent 252 dollars in singles disappearing down G-strings."*

"It's my ass, too, and Delilah explained that it was my heat and she destroyed the pictures."

"Yeah, okay, but remember, I'm watchin' you. Don't make me put you in time-out again."

"I'm gonna let that one go."

Thinking she might actually have won an argument, Freddie groaned, *"Well, shit."* Bright came back with, *"I can't. Just can't do it. If you, Winifred Lightfoot, lock me up again, I promise to take over your body, spend all your money on vibrators, and have them delivered to the Academy in a box marked 'open at assembly.'"*

"Okay, you win."

"Thank you."

With her own feet back on solid ground, Freddie was able to pace as she thought aloud. Walking back and forth, sometimes in circles, sometimes a square, and a couple times in perfect equilateral triangles, helped the way-beyond genius reason through any and all problems.

"So, before you 'duh'd' me, I was gonna say, in a somewhat freaked-out shriek, holy shit, are those militarized dino super soldiers?"

"To which I would've, once again, said, Duh."

"Right, moving past that..." Pulling another set of clothes out of her bag and putting on her *glassnoculars*, Freddie pressed the button on them and continued, *"They are upright, more humanoid, and those quads are definitely tyran-*

nosaurus in origin. At least as much as I can see below the frayed hems of those hand-me-down cut-off camos."

"Yep, I'll give you that," Bright readily agreed. *"And the arms are definitely iguanodon. Longer than a Rex, way more muscular. So, where the crap did all that thick, brown hair come from?"*

"I'm getting there," Freddie murmured. *"First, and it's right on the edge of my brain, those pinchers, the ones coming out of either side of their snouts... I've seen them... I know, I've seen... That's it!"* Fist pumping the air, she whooped, *"In* Scientific Phenomena Magazine, *a couple of months ago, there was an article about that dude that found a dinosaur-era spider. Those little sons of bitches had pincher-fangs just like those, but how... Whoa, what the hell?"*

Shocked into silence, unable to move, she watched as the now twenty dino mega soldiers stripped off their shirts in a ripple motion that would've made every group of football fans all over the world really, really jealous. Staring, eyes wide, hands clenched into tight fists at her side, Freddie gasped, *"And they've got the fucking armor?"*

"They've got what now?" Bright yelped. *"That's the what of the what?"*

"The armor of the dino-spider, natural, hard, calcified armor."

"That looks like a fucking tortoise's shell in black and gray?"
"Yep."

Then it hit her—the missing piece of the puzzle. There was only one thing that would explain the fur—not hair—on their arms and legs and the snout sticking out of their faces, the home of their venomous pincher-fangs.

"There's mane wolf mixed in with everything else."

"Are you fucking kidding?" Bright spat then, in a tiny bit gentler tone, asked, *"And what the hell is a mane wolf?"*

"New species, not really a wolf, not really a dog, stupid name, lives only in Brazil. They're meaner than a pissed-off black snake and eat everything they catch. Wonder where the... the... mad fucking scientist... deranged idiot... evil genius.... some or all of the above"—she shrugged—*"who created them got that DNA."*

"But you don't wonder where he got it from the prehistoric dino-spider with venomous pincher-fangs? What have I told you about priorities, Freddie? Wait! Where are we— Are we even gonna talk about the machine guns and swords they're carrying?"

Not taking the time to answer her alter ego's questions, figuring the winged tree grog would get the picture and/or just pick it out of her mind, Freddie did a spinning one-eighty. Sprinting to her compact, super light, magnificent jet that she was more thankful for than she would ever admit aloud because it would sound like she had a big head and nobody wanted people to think you were a snot, she was in the pilot's seat and ready to take off in record time.

Flipping the toggle switches and hitting the buttons, she grabbed ahold of the yoke with both hands and pulled back.

And nothing happened.

Over and over, again and again, Freddie tried, but not even the light on the radio would flicker. Back out of the cockpit with her handy-dandy toolbox, the more-than-capable, holding ten doctorates, and having more practical experience than most, Dr. Lightfoot stopped midstride.

Eyes glued to the enormous puddle of iridescent fluid running the entire length of her plane, she was just about to break the bad news to Bright when the winged tree frog growled through gritted teeth, *"If that's all our fuel, I'm disowning you for the rest of forever."*

"Well, you better call the Goddess and get the paperwork started, 'cause we're gonna be here for a while."

5

After the shortest strategy session in history, with Buck counting every damned second as the others discussed the next steps and how to locate Freddie, the "troops" were dispatched. Miranda and Chase headed back to FUC headquarters to head up the team there. Abe and Shauna headed to the Dragon Protection Agency to meet with other DPA Agents who were monitoring the coffee field fires, and apparently, Matt Firestone was on the way, too.

Abe said the dragon's experience with explosives would be invaluable. Buck thought it was just a way for his brother-in-law and his professor to talk shit about him. "But if it gets Freddie home safe, let 'em talk."

Pacing from one side of the bar to the other, the honey badger stopped on his fourth pass, pulled the phone out of his back pocket, and dialed the main switchboard at FUCN'A. Hitting the buttons to bypass the automated welcome BS, he hit number six for the infirmary/clinic and prayed.

Quicker than he could've ever guessed, the harsh,

clipped voice of Nurse Hetty Thomas barked, "Clinic. Speak."

Clearing his throat, trying to sound official while praying that she didn't ask his name, Buck requested, "Dr. Weathersbee, please?"

"Who's calling?"

Well, fuck! In for a penny, in for a pound…

Barking his words just like he'd done when training troops in some of the hottest pits of hell on earth for way too many years, Buck clipped, "This is Captain Blackthorne, Division Six, and when I want to be questioned, I will tell you so, Nurse Thomas. Is that clear?"

"Sir. Yes, sir," came the crow's immediate reply. "I'll get her right now, sir."

"See that you do."

The longer it took for the doctor to get on the phone, the more Buck was sure a dressing-down was in his very near future. Not only had he used his rank from before he retired but he'd given the name of the super classified, never-to-be-spoken-to-a-civvie Division Six.

"Fuck it. I'll tell them it was a matter of life or death and drastic measures were needed," he mumbled under his breath, still pacing a trench in the floor of the Sundowner.

Ready to hang up and find another way, a very high, obviously drunk, silly-as-the-day-is-long voice singsonged in his ear. "Helllllooooooooo, Dr. Weathers… Weathers… Weathers…" Overtaken by a bout of the giggles, the physician gasped then, with her words falling over each other, replied in one single breath. "This is me, the doctor, the person in charge of this clinic. The name's

Delilah, or it was. We've had an accident with the nitrous oxide, and I can't talk right now. Call back tomorrow." *Click.*

Jerking the phone from his ear and staring at the dark screen, Buck was dumbfounded. Had the world gone mad? Was he in an episode of *The Twilight Zone?* "Nope, *Candid Camera,*" he growled. "That's it, and this shit sucks."

Grabbing his leather jacket and keys, he hollered over his shoulder, "Talk to ya later, Mom," as he hit the doors of the Sundowner, stalking away at top speed.

After crossing the parking lot, the sound of gravel crunching under the heels of his boots, his leg was over the seat of his Harley, and the engine was rumbling when his mom's voice sounded in his head. *"I wondered what the hell you were waitin' on. Holler if you need us. I love you, son."*

"Love you, too, Mom."

Tearing out the back way, down the long lane that wound around the swamp, past his house, then Jack's, and finally Spencer's, Buck threw out his right foot as he took the last corner at top speed. Back upright in half a second, he squeezed the throttle and flew down the dirt road.

There was only one person who could help, one tiny, but mighty woman who'd fought by his side in more foxholes than he cared to remember. If there was anybody who could get him to Brazil with any hopes of finding his mate in time, it was her.

"Do I even know Freddie needs my help?"

"She needs our help," Harry snarled. *"Don't overthink, just do."*

"You're right, Har, but I'm not saying sir, yes sir. Ya hear?"

Pulling through the rusty gate that had been hanging

on the same single hinge since he was in grade school, Buck headed for the doublewide three-football-fields-long airplane hangar at the very back of the property. Grinning when he laid eyes on his oldest buddy and the first female to ever kick his ass, aside from his mother, Buck slid to a stop.

Turning the key off, he'd just hit the kickstand with the heel of his boot when Dusty's thick southern accent cut through the low fading rumble of his Harley. "What the hell you doin' here, boss? I heard tell y'all were up at some fancy Academy trainin' to be a super soldier."

"Yeah." He chuckled dryly. "Just too stupid to stay away from all that crap."

"Naw." Dusty quickly disagreed, her long blonde braids swinging as she shook her head. "Ya just got a big heart and a need to be the hero. I admire that."

"And I admire that you can fix anything with an engine and collect airplanes like most people collect dust bunnies under their bed."

Clapping her greasy hands, the sound muffled by a dirty red rag, the five-foot-nothing in human form, blonde-haired, blue-eyed, big-busted woman nodded. It was hard to believe that she shared her soul with a six-foot-six Rhode Island red hen who could peck a guy's eye out in half a second and could shoot a rifle like she was born with it in her wings. But it was as true as the day was long.

"So, you here to see my new toy?"

"Nope, I'm here to ask you to fly my ass to Brazil in your new toy."

"No shit?"

"No shit, Dusty." Not even taking a breath, just going for it and telling her the score, Buck walked right into the hangar with one of his best friends in the world instantly at his side. "I found my mate at that Academy." Holding up his hand as she started to speak, he forged ahead. "No time for congratulations, and I'm not so sure I deserve them… *yet.* To make a long story short, I had a slight malfunction showing off my skill in the explosives lab and found her in the clinic."

"Well, shit." Dusty snickered. "And you always wondered why we called you 'Go-Big-or-Go-Home Blackthorne.'"

Not stopping his forward motion or his explanation, the honey badger continued. "But she was gone before the drill-sergeant-turned-nurse was done with me." Scratching at the stubble on his jaw and stopping next to the modified jet, Buck cleared his throat. "Like an idiot, I waited until the next day when I was all healed up to go find her." Looking right at Dusty, he deadpanned, "You already figured out the rest. I know you. Grass doesn't grow under your feet. But I'll say it anyway. My mate was gone. Now, she's in trouble chasing some boogeyman in Brazil, and as far as I know, not one damned soul has been able to get ahold of her."

"You tried the whole mate-telepathy thing?"

"The what?"

Letting her head drop forward, her chin hitting her chest, Dusty groaned. "How is it that you can lead twenty soldiers into the desert, take down the enemy, save the civvies, and get everybody back home in one piece, but you'd forget your galdarned head if it wasn't attached?"

"'Cause I'm a man?"

Head popping up, a big smile on her face and a twinkle in her eyes that said Dusty was all in, the Rhode Island red pointed and chuckled. "Give that boy a gold star." Throwing her rag onto the rolling tool cart right beside her hip, she tapped her temple with the first two fingers of her left hand while unzipping her coveralls with the right. "Try using mind-to-mind communication. Some shifters are able to do it when they find their mates."

"I thought I had to have *been* with her first."

Out of her greasy overalls and standing before him in camouflage cargo pants and an olive-green T-shirt, Dusty mimicked his air quotes as she shook her head. "It's different for everybody, but you Blackthornes are faster than a one-legged man in a butt-kickin' contest and twice as strong. If anybody can make contact with that mate of yours, it's you, boss." Swatting him in the shoulder before turning around, Dusty added, "Now, get to callin' while I get Matilda here ready to go."

"Matilda?" No, it wasn't the time, but he just had to know. If there was one thing that was a constant in Buck's life, it was that Dusty had a story for absolutely everything.

"Yep." Patting the nose of her small, sleek creation, the Dusty Duster—or so Jack had said—the Rhode Island red looked over her shoulder, gave him a wink, and nodded. "Named her after my old auntie. You know the one we used to go visit on Fridays after school? With the..."

"With the old hound dog who never moved, the twenty-seven beehives, and the best molasses cookies ever baked?" Chuckling, despite the situation, he went on.

"Oh damn, she cussed like a sailor and smoked the tobacco she'd dried herself out of a corn cob pipe she carved with an old paring knife, didn't she?"

"That's her." Dusty nodded. "Well, Aunt Matilda fell off a ladder picking apples not long after you went back for another tour, and I stayed here to get the old place back together after Daddy died. God rest his soul. Matilda swore up and down that the doctors in the hospital up the road put her back together with pieces and parts from whatever they had lying around."

Laughing out loud, the sound echoing through the massive hangar and off the bodies of every plane and plane part all over the place, she slapped her leg and added, "Funny part was she was only in there 'cause we couldn't keep her in bed long enough to heal."

"You gotta be messin' with me."

"Nope, not even a little. Hell, she still lives in the same house with the same old dog. When we get back, I'll take ya over."

Nodding as she opened the hatch just in front of the wing on the very edge of the undercarriage, Buck caught sight of the words Dusty Door engraved on the handle. "That your design, too?"

"Sure is, boss," she answered with a grin. "Sold the Air Force the specs. It'll be on all the new fighter jets, my name, too."

"That's awesome."

"Yeah, I'm pretty pleased. Now, call that lady of yours and find out where we're headed. I'm gonna get this baby ready."

Suddenly nervous, unsure what to say or what kind of a reception he would receive, Buck did what he always did —took a leap of faith and prayed he came out the other end with his ass intact. *"Dr. Lightfoot?"*

When no answer came, he got a little louder. *"Winifred?"*

Still dead air, he griped, *"Hey, Har, you helpin'? It sure feels like I'm doin' this alone."*

"Oh, shut the hell up," his honey badger barked. *"I'm helpin', and you know it. Try again."*

"Umm, Freddie? You there?"

"Hell, yes, I'm here." Her voice was loud and clear, and more than a little pissed off. *"This is my head, dumbass. And if you're the mad mofo who created the dino super soldiers and burned up all my precious coffee beans, get the fuck out, tell your goon squad to stand down, and put your head between your legs and kiss your ass goodbye, 'cause I'm comin' for ya."*

Just like that, Buck was thrown out of Freddie's mind with a blast of magic that had him shaking his head and rubbing his ears. Turning back around just as Dusty slid from under the wing of the plane, the honey badger didn't even get his mouth opened before she asked, "Everything okay? You get a location?"

"I got us about half a location and one helluva headache."

"Ha!" Dusty barked with laughter. "Welcome to married life, boss."

6

"FREDDIE!"

"WHAT?!" she yelled right back to the winged tree frog perched inside her brain, who, at that very moment, was having a frenzy attack. *"What?! What?! What in all that's holy could be more important than fixing this—"* Throwing her hands in the air, she got as far *"Frikk.... ahhhhhhhhh, son of a biiiiitch!"* before gravity reared its ugly head.

Falling backward, her arms spinning like the blades of a windmill, her mouth opened as wide as it would go, and her eyes scrunched tight, Freddie's ass made immediate and painful contact with the rocky top of Mount Pedra da Mina with a thud, a crunch, and an "I'm gonna fu—"

"That was your mate. Our mate. The honey badger. Buck."

"—ckin'... Huh? What? That was my who?"

The last word was barely more than a whisper. Could Bright be right? Then the recent interaction with a deep sexy voice rumbling through her usually very attentive and astute brain resulting in the pitter-pat of her heart and the best little shiver she'd ever experienced dancing down her spine replayed in her mind.

Head falling backward onto the ground, her eyes still scrunched closed, her pleasingly plump badonkadonk hurting more than she was ever going to admit, Freddie squeaked out, *"That voice?"*

"Mmhmm."

"The one I yelled at?"

"Yep."

"The one I thought was the evil little shithead who destroyed the coffee fields for reasons we have yet to ascertain?"

"Sure enough."

"The one I threw outta my head and snapped my shields into place right behind, locking them tighter than Fort Knox and Granny's coin purse?"

"Yes, that would be the one."

"Then why didn't you stop me?"

"For the same reason I couldn't keep you from throwing your hands in the air, effectively tossing yourself off the side of your very own plane. I'm. Not. In. Control. Dipshit."

"Well, that was just uncalled for." Freddie sulked, slowly getting back to her feet. *"I'm entitled to a few mistakes. I am human, after all."*

"You only look human, but I get what you mean, and I think it was more than called for," Rainbow Bright sassed. *"You yelled at me first, and as long as we're counting mistakes..."*

"Yeah, well..." Dragging the toe of her Timberlands through the dirt and rocks, suddenly feeling guilty for being nasty to Bright and worried that she might have bitten off a little more than she could chew, Freddie apologized. *"I'm sorry for yelling. And I'll cop to a few not*

completely thought-out ideas on this mission. You were right. Yeah, I said it. Do not make me regret it. It was a dick move, not bringing backup. But I have no idea how that hole got in the fuel line, and the battery is suddenly dead. We didn't hit anything in the air or otherwise. I am an excellent pilot, you know that, and I tripled checked everything in preflight."

"And Willem has inspected this plane more times than even I can count."

"Yeah, that, too."

Hurrying on before her alter ego could gain any steam or whip up another comeback, Freddie quickly changed the subject. Staring over the ledge at the platoon of dino super soldiers, she said, "What do you think they're waiting on? I know they know we're up here. The big one at the front there." She pointed with her elbow, trying to act coy. "The one with the almost cool mohawk and the tattoo on his forearm..."

"Yeah, I see him," Bright snapped. "As we've discussed ad nauseam, you and I share a brain and eyes and—"

"Yeah, well, he keeps looking right at us." Spinning around on her toes and pointing at her jet with both hands in a somewhat manic flinging motion, she excitedly exclaimed, "He can see through this smoke just like I can, like you can, like everybody can. And I bet the smell of coffee isn't making him jones for a quad shot espresso right now."

"I'm sure you're right, but we need to..."

"Why didn't I make a Wonder Woman plane?" Freddie blurted out, needing to finish her thought. There were times, not many but a few, when rambling on about nonsense helped her come to a conclusion that would have otherwise been missed. She prayed that a convoluted bit of logic would prevail on this occasion.

"What was I thinking? Invisibility. That's what it needs to be perfect. Then no one would ever know where we were." Huffing out an exasperated breath, she growled under her breath before continuing. *"It's not like those scaly monstrosities could miss a jet, even one as small and compact as mine, sitting like the world's biggest paperweight, is it? Hell no! They have to have seen it. Smoke or no smoke, at the very least, Dino Dave zeroed his beady black peepers in on it. He's been scoping us out since they first popped out of that jungle over there. Bet he's the one who lit the fuse. Had to be him. It's always the big, tough ones."*

"Beady black peepers?"

"Yeah, that's what I said."

"You also said that all the bad guys were little, but those patchwork dinosaurs aren't little."

"I said, if you recall correctly, that the guy in charge is always little in the way that count."

Spinning back around, her arms flapping like the wings she didn't have at the moment, her voice getting a little too shrieky for even her own ears, Freddie kept right on ranting. *"And back on their eyes. Of course, they have beady black peepers. What other color eyes would they have? Brown, green, gorgeous blue with little flecks of gold that swirl when he's embarrassed like—"*

"Like your mate? The one you screamed at like a banshee and banished from your mind? Those blue eyes?"

"Okay, I said I was sorry. Can you try to play nice, at least until we get home? And while I'm asking for favors, can you tell

me how that sexy hunka-hunka honey badger got into my brain?"

"Oh, Freddie Freddie Freddie Freddie." Bright tsk'd, the sound making the woman think about putting the winged tree frog in time-out again, but this time for a year or two. *"For a smart chick, you can be all kinds of stupid sometimes."*

"Well, thank you ever so much, Rainbow Bright, Princess Pain in My Ass, for the commentary on my lack of practical knowledge in the field of mating. As you might recall, I was as sure as someone with ten Ph.D.s, an M.D., and an IQ as high as mine can be that I would never ever never in a million, trillion years find my mate."

"Yes, and if you recollect, I told you that there is someone for everyone, even you."

"Yes, but..."

"Yes, but what?"

"Yes, but... well, I don't have an answer. Just tell me how to use the Jedi mate mind-link thingy. Is that too much to ask?"

"No, it's really not, but..."

"Yeah, what now?"

"You remember Dino Dave?"

"Yeah, I was the one who named him." For sure, her tone was snarky, and, yes, she was being a bitch, but things had gone from bad to worse and were quickly heading to "bite me in the ass and call me Betsey" territory.

"Well, he's leading the march toward the base of the mountain. And if I'm not mistaken, those things in their hands, or paws, or claws, are motorized grappling hooks attached to long-barrel air rifles that are not for shooting cute T-shirts with cool sayings on them into the crowds of adoring fans that they most assuredly do not have."

Spinning one way and then the other before sprinting forward, throwing herself on the ground, and sliding to the edge like she was stealing home, Freddie peered over the edge. Sure enough, there they were. *"Why did I have to ask? Why didn't I keep my mouth shut? Why didn't I fix the plane? Why do I always put the most horrible things out in the universe just daring Destiny and her even worse sister, Fate, to bite me in the ass?"*

"Why aren't you calling your mate?"

"Oh, shut up, Bright, you know why."

"Are we going with pride or stupidity?"

"I'm going with, when the hell have we ever needed anyone to save us? We are tree frog..."

"Butterfly, fairy princess, and witch..."

"Yeah, hear us fuckin' roar."

Up on her feet and racing back to the jet, Freddie then jumped into the cockpit, used the yoke to catapult across the pilot's seat, and flew through the cabin like she'd been shot out of a cannon. Opening compartments, lockers, closets, and cubbyholes as she went, the renowned researcher ended the first leg of her sprint by grabbing the handles in the very center of the back wall and flinging open the gun cabinet.

"I'll need this, this, this and this." Grabbing the rocket launcher, the one that fired canisters designed to rain silver nitrate pellets in a four-hundred-yard-radius, a case of grenades loaded with silver-laced gunpowder, her shoulder harness with all seven of her finest silver blades, and the one and only LF623 Minigun—a machine gun of her own design—the Lightfoot623 (Her last name and her birth date) with the capability of firing 10,623 rounds per minute.

"*But you only have two hands,*" Bright pointed out.

"*Watch and learn, Princess Poo Poo,*" Freddie growled. "*Watch and learn.*"

Back out of the plane the way she'd come, Freddie placed the shoulder harness right behind the wheel on the pilot's side. Twenty yards away, between two huge boulders, the back with a divot the size of her backside and the front with the perfect flat edge, she set up the Minigun on its tripod. Fifty yards closer, just about halfway to the edge, she pulled the retractable spade from her backpack, dug a trench, and placed all twenty-four grenades in a nice neat line.

Running through the plan one more time in her head, the mechanical whir of the dino super soldiers' climbing contraptions buzzed through the air. Listening to the *thwap* and *clank* of the hooks making contact with the ledge right below, Freddie got down on her knees behind a pile of grass-covered rocks. Balancing the front of the rocket launcher on the peak of the heap, she set her ass on her heels and the butt of the weapon on her shoulder.

Breathing in as deeply as she could to the count of three, Freddie held it for an extra second before exhaling to the exact same count, only backward. "Three... two... one..."

Listening to the all-too-familiar scrape of combat boots against rock, all she could do was wait. They were coming. There was no doubt about it. The dino super soldiers were coming to get her.

"*And I still don't know who is behind this shit or what's*

really going on," she whispered to Bright. *"Guess we have to keep at least one of these mofos alive to get our answers."*

Not waiting for an answer, Freddie kept her eyes trained on the edge. She heard the dinos' boots on the outcropping just below. Then the pfft of the air rifle cut through the air. Next came the *thwap* of the high-tension wire. And lastly, the *chink* and *thunk* right before the bright flash of four hooks simultaneously dug into the ledge right in front of her.

Finger on the trigger, she inhaled slowly, focused on Bright's whispered, *"Steady, Freddie. You got th—"*

"Owwww…" Freddie screamed, her right hand flying off the trigger, slapping on her neck, batting away the instant and horrendous stinging and burning.

Slumping backward, her arms suddenly full of lead and her legs like two of those Styrofoam noodles she'd seen kids beat each other with while in the pool of every hotel she'd ever stayed in, Freddie fell into the waiting arms of none other than Dino Dave. Squinting against the glare of the sun and the effects of whatever he'd shot into her neck, the mohawked dino super soldier was almost handsome in a bad-guy-just-drugged-her kinda way.

Working hard to stay awake and not to be taken hostage, Freddie's muscles turned to jelly and her brain to mush. All she could do was slur, "You didn't play fair, you…" before everything faded to black.

7

"Dive! Dive! Dive!" Buck roared, throwing off his seatbelt and both over-the-shoulder harnesses before vaulting over the center console and racing to the back of the modified jet. Shoving his arms into the straps of his parachute, he slid open the side door and grabbed ahold of the handle.

"Closer," he snapped, waiting until the bottom of the plane brushed the treetops before bellowing, "I'm out! See ya on the ground!"

Knowing Dusty had his back, without waiting for a response, Buck jumped from the plane. They didn't need words. They'd been in stickier situations. That Rhode Island red would do what she had to do to keep them all alive.

"Just like you're gonna do," Harry barked. *"Can't you fall any faster? That son of a bitch knows the terrain. We're gonna lose him. When did you start falling like an old lady?"*

"How about I let you handle this, General Jerkoff?"

No sooner were the words out of his mouth than the

honey badger with whom he shared his soul forced the shift. One minute, Buck was watching his unconscious mate being carried through the Brazilian jungle, thrown over the shoulder of the freakiest-looking dinosaur nobody in the swamp would ever believe existed, and the next, his perspective was that of a passenger in Harry's mind.

"What the...?"

"Be careful what you wish for," the honey badger spat. *"You know you don't have to ask me twice, butthead. I have control issues that there just ain't no cure for."*

"Yeah, okay, just don't hit that tree," Buck quipped, trying hard not to laugh out loud. *"I'd hate to have to tell everybody you got a bump on your noggin' while playing George of the Jungle in the jungle."*

"Shut up," Harry growled. *"Nobody likes a back-of-the-mind paratrooper."*

Laughing despite the situation, happier than he would ever admit to his alter ego to being in the seven-foot, fur-covered body of the roughest, toughest honey badger the world had ever known, Buck focused on Freddie.

Letting his eyes slide closed, Blackthorne followed the glowing stream of light, the precious gossamer strand of magic that joined his soul to his mate's. He wouldn't let her get away. There was no way in hell the fucker who had her would be allowed to hurt her.

"Holy crap, Buck, you see that shit?" Harry snarled. *"That bastard's headin' underground."*

Pulling the cord in his left paw, disconnecting the shoot from the line, Harry barked, *"Hold on to your ass, son.*

The landing's gonna be bumpy," at precisely the same time that Buck screamed, *"We're too high!"*

Holding his breath, the sound of Harry's face taking a severe beating from tree branches, stalks of bamboo, and vines thicker than his forearms, Buck refused to lose sight of Freddie. *"Twist your hips to the left and your shoulders to the right,"* he yelled. *"It'll turn us out of these fucking vines and away from the fangs of that snake right there."*

"What snake?" Harry yelled before immediately roaring, *"Son of a bitch, that's a big fuckin' snaaaaaaaaaaaaake!"*

Laughing out loud, knowing that the only thing in the whole freakin' world his honey badger feared was snakes, Buck had to add, *"How the hell can you be scared of snakes? You eat them like queso and chips, for cripes' sake. Don't even need a beer to wash them down. It just makes no sense, Har. You're so far above them on the food chain they can't even see your ass."* Sadly, there was no time to wait for Harry's reply, as they were suddenly close enough to count the scales on the snake's belly.

"Turn! Turn! Turn!" Buck shouted.

Narrowly missing the open maw of a huge, bright green anaconda, Harry spat, *"No shit! I'm turnin'! I'm turnin'! I'm turnin'! You just keep your eyes on Freddie and leave the falling to me. Can you still see her?"*

"Yeah, but the signal"—tapping his temple, Buck stressed —*"is gettin' way too faint. The son of a bitch is going deeeeeeeeep! Real deep. We're gonna have to— Watch out!"*

Grunting right along with his honey badger, Buck was suddenly in the dark as Harry closed his eyes tight, tucked his chin to his chest, and curled his massive, muscular body into a tight ball a split second after his huge back paws hit the soft mossy ground. Rolling through the jungle like a bowling ball through pins, Blackthorne held his breath while forcing every ounce of strength he possessed into his alter ego.

"Don't you dare kill us! Why do I ever let you take the lead?"

Stopping with a thud and thunk, it was immediately followed by Harry's whooped, *"Now, that's how you jump out of a perfectly good plane!"*

Buck did not share his honey badger's sentiment. He was just happy to be alive, on the ground, and that much closer to his mate.

"Whatever you say, big guy. Now get your ass off the ground and head back the way we just came."

Not needing any more encouragement, Harry sprang upward, hit the ground on the balls of his feet, and cut through the dense foliage like a knife through hot butter. *"Lead the way, hotshot,"* he commanded. *"I've got the accelerator. You've got the steering wheel."*

Maneuvering through the jungle, following his mate's trail, Buck could hear the sounds of water, the skittering of smaller animals through the trees and across rocks, and blessedly, the engine of Dusty's plane making its descent. *"Our girl's found a place to land close by."*

"Good for her." Harry barely acknowledged him. *"You just worry about finding me the entrance to that asshole's underground lair."*

"Lair?" Buck asked. *"Did this dino just become a supervillain in a comic book you are never gonna write?"*

"No, asshole, he's the dick that has our mate," Harry growled. *"And what exactly would you call the place where the ugliest muthafuckin' dino we've ever laid eyes on calls home?"*

"*Good point.*"

"*Yeah, I thought you'd agree.*"

"*Keep going. He's in that patch of trees on the other side of that smoldering field.*"

"Could you be a little more specific?" Harry growled. "There's about ten-thousand miles of smoldering coffee fields in the immediate vicinity."

"*The one straight ahead, smartass.*"

"That's Mr. Smartass to you."

"*I'll try to remember that.*"

Needing to concentrate, his mental bond with Freddie being pulled to its tenuous limit, Buck summoned every ounce of magic he could without using any of Harry's and thought about the first time he'd recognized her scent. Holding tight to the sweet, citrusy fragrance of verbena and the crisp, clean aroma of a spring rain, their connection glowed with a renewed vigor.

Next came the picture he and Olivia had pulled up on the computer. Sure, it was only an ID photo, but even that was gorgeous. Bright green eyes with just the tiniest ring of red, fluffy black curls that he just knew would feel like silk running through his fingers, and a perfectly curvy figure his hands were itching to get ahold of.

In his younger years, that was all Buck would've needed to chase that winged tree frog, capture her with his charm, and have his wicked way with her, but this was different. This was the big time. Forever with the woman made for him by the Universe and the Great Goddess. Looks were important, but it was Freddie's heart and soul that mattered even more.

Reading her file, something he hadn't bothered to tell

Chase or Miranda for fear they'd have him booted out of FUCN'A on his ass, Buck couldn't have been more impressed. Everything Freddie did, every project she worked on, every invention she thought up and brought to life, just everything she did, was for the betterment of the environment. She believed in the advancement of every paranormal race and wanted to keep humans safe. Heck, she was a superhero with webbed feet and stunning rainbow wings.

Laughing, he mumbled, *"She doesn't just want a better world. My mate is ready to make that shit happen."*

"She really is something," Harry agreed. *"And she's as warm-blooded as you and me. Not one thing to stop us from being with her forever, not one thing at all."*

"Bet I can make her hot-blooded. Wanna put a twenty on it?"

"Get your head back in the game, son. Find me an entrance 'cause the bottom of my paws are about to burn off if we don't run outta real estate first."

"Stop right here," Buck snapped, the glowing bond he shared with Freddie flashing and pulsing like the neon atop an all-night tattoo parlor. *"We're right on top of her."*

"I'm gonna let that go." Harry chuckled. *"But you better revisit the whole 'being on top of her' as soon as you can."*

"Dude," Buck scolded, just barely holding back his own chuckle. *"Holster that libido. Weren't you the one just raggin' on me about the same damned thing? Pick a side, old man. Not only will a hard-on get in the way, but I know how you get when you're turned on, and I'm gonna need you focused."*

"Yeah, well, if you hadn't been on a sex strike for the last year, maybe I wouldn't be a horny honey badger."

Ignoring the same argument they'd been having for the last eleven months, Buck didn't need to tell Harry he now knew why he hadn't been interested in any other women for over a year and had turned down dates left and right. It was obvious. It was nature's way of getting him ready to find his mate.

"It's got to be..." Zeroing in on the one thing that didn't belong, the piece of landscape that was just too green, too bright, too perfect, he yelled at precisely the same moment as Harry, *"There it is!"*

Holding on as the honey badger flew a hundred yards to the fake plant, Buck focused on the concrete and metal right below. *"There's a huge, completely vertical shaft, like a silo, right beneath us and then a labyrinth of tunnels snaking out in every direction from there."*

Throwing open the lead lid—bigger than a manhole and twice as heavy—Harry's foot had just landed on the first rung of the ladder when the whistle of a yellow-throated warbler reached Buck's ear. Returning the birdcall with the song of a Louisiana water thrush, he told his honey badger, *"Hang on. That's Dusty."*

"Yeah, I know. Did you forget I've been with ya since day one?"

"No, asshole. I wasn't... oh, forget it."

Appearing at the edge of the dense overgrown foliage surprisingly untouched by the fires, her face, covered in black and green greasepaint and her blonde hair tucked up in a black nylon beanie, only Dusty's smile was visible. Holding up her right hand, she signaled with two fingers that she was going left and around the other side. With a single nod, Buck approved her plan and watched his oldest friend disappear into the jungle.

"Guess she found another way in," he mused to Harry as the honey badger made quick work of the long, steep ladder.

"Yep," came Harry's clipped reply. *"Now, which way?"*

"North about 100 paces then right fifty more."

Traveling so quickly that the walls of the dark gray tunnel were nothing more than a blur to Buck, Harry snorted sarcastically. *"Just for shits and giggles, you got an estimate on the number of bad guys we're about to run into?"*

"Thirty, maybe thirty-five heartbeats right ahead. More spread out all over," Buck answered back. *"Can't you hear them?"*

"Not even a little. Feels like I got wool in my ears," Harry responded, his tone sounding weird, somehow off and distant, all the usual playful piss and vinegar reduced to little more than a bad attitude.

"You okay, big guy?"

"I'm... not... well..."

And just like that, Harry was face down on the floor and Buck was trapped inside his seven-foot, fur-covered honey badger's body. Trying to force the shift, throwing everything he had—magically and otherwise—into getting them both back into his human body, the best Buck could do was turn Harry's head to the side.

Well, shit, that took way more energy than it should have. At least I can see and smell, he thought to himself. *And what is that?*

It took a second longer than it should have, but then again, he'd never been trapped inside his honey badger without a way out before. There was no denying it. The steady, approaching footsteps of ten, maybe fifteen big-ass dinos were heading straight for his location.

Wake up, Harry, he ordered. *Wake the fuck up. Now is not the time. You have to...*

"It's no use," a deep rasping grumble growled from just above his head. "Your honey badger's down for the count, and you're trapped. Just shut up and enjoy the ride, Buck Blackthorne. The boss has been waiting for you."

The boss?

Buck felt the prick of a needle in the side of Harry's neck.

Hey, what the fuuuuuuu....?

Vision blurring, his words slurred together, Buck felt like the morning after a ten-day drunk—bad with a capital B.

"Don't fight it," the growl ordered, a weird sense of regret in his tone. "It'll just make the hangover worse, and where you are going, you're gonna need a clear head. At least when you wake up, I can assure you that you'll be you again and honey badger will still be sleeping."

Yeah, well, fu— fu— fu...

And that was as far as he got.

8

Unfortunately, waking up chained to a chair wasn't new for Freddie. Neither were the silver shackles burning the skin on her wrists and ankles. Being in her bra and panties with all ten tootsies in two feet of water with jumper cables attached to long, scary-looking bolts coming out of her cuffs? Now that was a whole new experience.

Blinking back the effects of the drug Dino Dave had injected into her veins, she called to her alter ego, praying Raeanna was okay. *"Hey, Bright, you in there? You good?"*

"Yes, I'm here," the winged tree frog slowly replied, her voice hollow, almost tinny. *"Good? Not even close."*

"What the hell happened?"

A low moaning sigh followed by a deep, stuttering breath, and Bright's whispered answer, sans any sass, was, *"That fucking dino outsmarted us. Apparently, he knew another way up the mountain that we didn't see."*

"Yeah," Freddie spat. *"I'm such a fucking idiot. Why didn't I—"*

"*Stop that shit,*" Bright hissed, even her rebuke sounding weak. "*I didn't think of it either. All th— that— *cough-wheeze* matters, is fi- finding out what's going on and getting us outta here.*"

Suddenly swamped with worry and more fear than she'd felt in a really long time, Freddie demanded, "*What's wrong, Bright? I can't tell anything about what's going on with you. Can barely even feel you at all. What is happening?*"

Silence. Cold, barren. Deafening. That was all Freddie got in return.

Pushing the magic from her mom's witchy side and the fairy enchantment from her dad, the mysticism she usually let her winged tree frog control, Freddie kept calling. "*Bright, damn you. Do not do this to me right now. Yes, I operate better under pressure, but this is bullshit. Utter and complete bullshit.*" More magic. More power. More of everything she had, and Freddie started screaming, "*Raeanna Bree, you better answer me. Now is not the time for the silent treatment. Especially when I wasn't being the tiniest bit bitchy. You need to answer me NOW! YOU NEED—*"

CLAP!

CLAP!

CLAP!

Slow applause reverberated off the concrete walls all around her, forcing Freddie to swallow the rest of the frantic orders she was about to shout at her alter ego. Throwing her mind open as far and as wide as it would go, she instantly zeroed in on a blank spot. A little bit of nothing amid a hive of activity and mysticism.

There were shifters, all the same somehow. It was

weird. And there was the bastard, Dino Dave. Oh, yeah, he was there.

"I'm coming for you, asshole," she ground out through gritted teeth, her every malicious intent pointed at Dino Dave. "That's a promise."

"Oh, I don't think you'll be going anywhere, Dr. Winifred F. Lightfoot, renowned scientist, highly regarded researcher, most sought-after authority on prehistoric lifeforms, and so many other things including—"

A loud clearing of the throat, which carried so much sarcasm Freddie thought she might just choke on it, filled the cavern. It was stifling, pompous, and reminded her of someone. She was sure of it. But who?

Then the mysterious voice started again, and the breadcrumbs of clues Freddie was following through the supercomputer housed in her little gray cells went *poof!*

"Furry." Another clap. "United." Yet another of the same, this one with more oomph. "Coalition." Well, shit, more applause, and Freddie was sure she'd get a bighead. Sadly, the most recent was laced with more than a hint of evil, dirty, black magic that bit and stung every inch of her exposed skin. "Agent."

"Okay, so you know me. How about you come out and introduce yourself? We can have some tea, maybe a scone. You like scones? I can take them or leave them, but from the hint of an accent in your voice, I kinda think you might like them."

She knew that voice. Had felt that magic before or, at the very least, something very close to it. Where and when was still a mystery. But why did she feel like it hadn't always been so nasty and filled with hate? Those were the questions her still-foggy brain was having trouble answering.

And if there's one thing that's sure to drive me absolutely batty, it's a question I can't answer or a puzzle I can't solve...

"No, I don't think I will," the voice mocked, its nasally, grating, irritating pitch making the hairs on Freddie's arms stand on end and little goosebumps dance the Macarena up and down her spine.

"Who the fuck is this?" It was driving her mad.

"Instead, how about we play a little game of show and tell?"

"And if I don't want to play?"

"One of two things will happen," the voice mocked. "My... What cutesy little moniker did you come up with for them again?" A tension-filled pause preceded a caustically sarcastic, "Ummmm?"

At which time, Freddie imagined the idiot who was trying to be the world's next supervillain to be tapping his or her—'cause she honestly couldn't tell if the asshole was male or female—finger on his or her chin. "Ah, yes," followed by a snap of said fingers and a dry chuckle that did nothing to calm Freddie's nerves. "Dino super soldiers." Wildly clapping, the voice shouted, "Brava! Brava!" As quickly as it had started, the applause ended, leaving only echoes in its wake as the voice's snide diatribe continued. "Very inventive, although I do admit to expecting way more from you, Dr. Lightfoot. I mean, after following your career from its very beginning, from your very first walk across the very first stage to receive your very first degree, I just... Well, that's what happens when you meet someone so famous in person..."

After a round of mocking tsk's, which had Freddie promising to make the asshole's beatdown take an hour longer than she'd initially planned, the person auditioning for the world's next supervillain sighed. "It's always a disappointment. Anyway, one of my guard, as I like to call them, will flip a switch, and this will happen."

Instantly flooded with enough electricity to keep at least the south end of the Vegas Strip going until dawn on New Year's Eve, Freddie shook and shuddered as current after current of raw power coursed through her veins. Refusing to pass out, her eyes glued to the null spot in the massive shield engulfing the whole underground facility, Freddie thought about Bright. She thought about her friends and about FUC and, most importantly, about Buck Blackthorne.

Nails biting into her palms, her toes curling toward her arches, Freddie knew she would be glowing in the dark for more than a month when the flow of voltage just stopped. Sadly, the jumping and quaking of Freddie's muscles did not. Neither did the way her jaw clenched, nor the rolling of her eyes to the back of her head.

SLAP!

The bone-shattering swat of a meaty paw across her jaw had Freddie's eyes flying open and her roar of, "You will fucking die for that, dickhead!" flying out of her mouth before she could stop it.

"Nope, not me, Dr. Lightfoot." The voice chuckled. "Either you or..."

The whir of a small motor and the sound of metal

scraping metal filled the large room as a curtain on the opposite side, one she hadn't realized was there until that very moment, slowly slid open. Her heart ceased to beat. The breath froze in her lungs. Her worst nightmare was staring her in the face, and there wasn't a damn thing she could do about it. Spread-eagle, hanging from silver chains and shackles just like her own, the gorgeous muscles of his arms and legs stretched to their limit, was her mate, the one and only Buck Blackthorne.

"You better not touch a hair on his—"

Slap!

Another blow across the face. This one harder, the sting emanating down both sides of Freddie's neck into her shoulders and skittering down her spine.

Eyes flying to the dino super soldier standing at her side, she gasped. Seeing pain and fear, genuine regret in the deep, dark depths of his black beady eyes, it was all she could do not to ask what was wrong. Then she remembered the hypodermic needle in the neck, the silver eating away at the skin on her wrists and ankles, and the electricity still making her feel a little twitchy, and Freddie wanted to rip off his arms and beat him with them.

Have to think. Have to think. Have to make sure nothing happens to Buck. Have to make sure Bright is okay. Have to figure out who is doing this and why. Have to use my brain. Can't be emotional. Have to be practical. This is a problem. And who's better at solving problems than you, Freddie?

"Fucking nobody," she mumbled under her breath.

Inhaling deeply, sure what she was about to do was going to earn her, at the very least, another wallop but more than likely more voltage whipping through her body, Freddie exhaled slowly. Snorting with sarcastic snickers, she taunted, "Okay, so I give. What's your supervillain name?"

Not waiting for an answer, needing to force her captive's hand, sure she could coerce the idiot to make a mistake that she would use to her advantage, Freddie chuckled. "Let me guess, Voltage Vixen?"

When no answer came, Freddie tilted her head to the side, looked up at the ceiling like she was thinking really hard, and hummed, "No, wait, I've got it. Coffee Killing King! That's it, isn't it?"

Pop! Slap! Whap!

The three-for-one hurt like a son of a bitch. Her jaw was on fire and most definitely dislocated—if not broken—from a punch, followed by an open-handed slap, and then one hell of a backhand, but they hadn't touched Buck. That was what was important. Her hunka-hunka, hot-as-hell honey badger was still unscathed.

One quick inhale and a quick jerk of her jaw, followed by a squishy pop and crack that she refused to examine too closely, and Freddie was able to come back with, "Okay, those were clearly not your favorite. How about you come on out and let me see if you're an evil boy asshole or an evil girl asshole? Then I'll have some better options for you."

Once again, the silence was deafening. Regrettably, there was a glaring difference, something that made Freddie sick to her stomach and her heart try to jump right out of her chest. The big blob of nothingness, the null spot amid all the magic and activity in the underground hive, the asshole who had orchestrated the giant pile of horseshit she presently found her pleasingly plump badonkadonk swimming in—almost literally— was moving toward Buck.

Scrambling to come up with anything that would get the asshole talking again, to get her captor to stop moving toward her mate and come after her, Freddie shrieked, "Hey, how about Beanhead Bozo? Or Brazilian Banana-in-the-Tailpipe Licker? Or... or... or..."

Sucking in more air than her lungs could ever hold as the person responsible for the destruction of her beautiful coffee beans, her own capture, and, most importantly, her sexy hot-ass honey badger being strung up for target practice came into view, Freddie roared, "Son of a bitch! You have got to be kidding me. I thought you were dead."

Pow! Slap! Bam!

Unscathed, except for a splitting headache that no amount of ibuprofen would ever, in her very long life-time, conquer, Freddie glared with all the venom she could muster. Quite a lot if she did say so herself.

Refusing to look away even as the four-foot-eleven—if she hadn't been wearing those god-awful black, patent-leather, five-inch stiletto-heeled platform shoes—waste of space from Freddie's past scowled like she was the freakin' Queen of Hearts, the winged tree frog seriously thought about sticking out her tongue and singsonging, "Nanny-nanny-booboo." But she didn't.

Inhaling deeply, not at all surprised to see that her childhood nemesis—tales of whose death were greatly exaggerated—still had the same gross-beyond-words brassy, bleach-blonde shoulder-length stick-straight hair and hadn't gained an ounce to add even the slightest curve to her thin-as-a-rail figure. The black pleather catsuit assured no one missed that the cuckoo-for-cocoa-puffs bitch could've been a stand-in for a fence post at any given moment. It was the weird way the bump on the bridge of her nose and the hook at the end had gotten even more pronounced that seemed to defy logic.

If the crazy-even-when-she-was-young-and-had-most-assuredly-gone-all-the-way-off-the-deep-but-still-had-a-brain insect shifter had been able to fund and build the underground "hive" Freddie found her pleasingly plump badonkadonk being held in, why hadn't the weirdo gotten her nose fixed? Heck, plastic surgery for shifters of any kind was a breeze. Kicked-up healing abilities made recovery time nearly nothing. It was definitely a mystery Freddie would have to think about *after* she kicked the bitch's ass for daring to lay a finger on her mate.

She had bigger fish to fry, and in Freddie Lightfoot's world, that meant snarling through gritted teeth, "And tell your fucking dino henchman to stop hitting me, Zenobia, or I'll rip that stinger right outta your ass and beat ya both senseless with it."

With his head feeling like a fuzzy bowling ball, his gut twisting in on itself, and the muscles in his arms and legs on fire, Buck was sure the end of the world as he knew it was just around the corner. Then some shrieking harpy started yelling right beside his ear, and he wondered if killing her would be considered justifiable homicide.

Ready to open his eyes and tell the screaming banshee exactly what he thought of her, something in the very back of his foggy brain, a little voice, well, more of a scratchy grumble, whispered, *"Don't do it. Just listen. Listen... and remember."*

Remember what?

Absolutely, without a doubt, Buck was sure he was supposed to know what was going on. He just had to decide if the little voice in the back of his head was real or a very vivid figment of his imagination. Then something the wailing wretch next to him shrieked cleared his mind in a fraction of a second.

"You are such a piece of work, Winifred Lightfoot. A real—"

"My. Name. Is. Freddie."

Holy shit on a shingle, it was his mate. She was alive. She was safe. She was here.

But where was *here*?

Doing what he'd been trained to do, what he would be kicking himself later for not doing the first half a second he was coherent, Buck opened his enhanced senses as wide as he could. Letting the mystical fingers of the magic given to him by the Great Goddess, the retired marine captain quickly got the lay of the land.

Number one, and a real pain in the ass, was the heavy shroud of black magic and nasty wards blocking him from talking to Harry. It was a wall, a thick, inky, oily, sticky wall that stung if he metaphorically touched it and tried to infect his senses with its own creepy tendrils. But it wasn't all sorcery. Oh, hell no, that would've been too easy. There was technical shit in there. Mechanical and electrical rigmarole keeping him from getting his honey badger's help and using a drop of their combined strength or magic.

Number two, the technical, mechanical, electrical bullshit served two purposes. One he knew was keeping not only him but his feisty mate on lockdown and from shifting. The berserk, bellowing banshee still bitching not two inches from his ear was apparently not as stupid as she sounded. Pity. Stupid bad guys—make that stupid bad women—were so much easier to deal with. Nope, this cuckoo-for-cocoa-puffs crazy had hidden its other purpose. Tucked it away deep inside the thick rock of the earth itself. Was it defensive? Was it for her weirdo experiments? Had she created the dino super soldiers? Hell, they all looked alike. Maybe she was lonely. If she bitched at everybody like she was yelling at Freddie, well, then it was a good bet she had to invent her own playmates.

Number three, he needed to stop trying to be Sherlock Holmes and listen to what the hell was happening right in front of him. Freddie was there. She was pissed. And she obviously had a history with Crazy-ass Screaming Bitch, as he'd unaffectionately named their captor. There were at least a thousand heartbeats in the spindly tunnels snaking out for miles all around him. Too many to take on with any hope of living through the experience. He would have to find another way, and that meant praying to the Goddess that he could somehow communicate with his mate.

Oh, there was also a number four. The last, but also the freakiest thing he'd found during his brief mental reconnaissance, every single one of the thousand or so heartbeats were all beating in unison. One, strong, *thump thump thump* that made the hair at the back of his neck stand on end and his inner soldier ask what the fuckity fuck weirdo shit was happening there.

Tuning to Madame Crazy-ass to his right, Buck was just in time to hear, "So, you think you deserve an answer? You think you're something special, don't you, Winifred? Someone people should bow to? Better than the rest of us? That's it, isn't it, Winifred? You have a question, so the world should stop turning and get you an answer. Is that it? Come on, Winifred."

"My name is Freddie."

"At least try to be honest. Winifred. Winifred. Winifred. Wini—"

"Holy shit, Zenobia, grow the hell up," Freddie snapped, the tone of her voice telling Buck that she was ready to go homicidal winged tree frog all over this Zenobia chick, and damn it all to hell, he really wanted to open his eyes and watch.

But you can't... You have to... You have to... Aww, fuck, what is it that I have to do?

Once again pulled out of his inner monologue, Buck wanted to laugh out loud when Freddie sassed, "Didn't you hear? We're old now. Not kids. Not in high school anymore. You're not a mean girl, and I don't wear glasses. We're women. We do not handle our shit like this."

The rattle of chains told Buck that his mate was as trussed up as he was and just as pissed. Then she growled, "And I promise you one thing, you stupid little yellow jacket, I will knock the stripes right off your backside the first chance I get. You are—"

"I. Am. In. Control." The satisfied, cocky purr was too much to handle. He couldn't hold back anymore. He needed to...

"You... ne-ne-need..." Barely audible, struggling to breathe, let alone speak, the voice at the farthest back corner of his mind whispered, *"The – Th-the dev-device."* A stuttering gasp, the pain almost palpable, it added, *"Bite— bite down."*

What the literal fuck was going on? How was there another voice, not Harry's and not Freddie's, in his mind? Who was giving him instructions? Could they be trusted? Could he...

"Yes! I fucking think I deserve to know why you blew up all the coffee fields in Brazil and why you burned out huge portions of the rainforest and injured the environment and killed all the little critters. Are you planning to do it to all the coffee fields all over the world? Are you seriously that deranged? Did you not get the cuddles you needed? Did you lose your favorite dolly? Oh, and, for the love of all things holy, why the fuck did you use wolfsbane, and why the fuck am I here?'

Cackling laughter filled the entire cavern, bouncing off the rock walls, smacking Buck in the face, assaulting his ears with its high, piercing, grating wail. "Oh, Winifred, you do so amuse me," the bitch wheezed, her maniacal laughter waning while her sarcasm got thicker. "But then again, you always have. Remember that time in high school?"

"What time, Zenobia? We were there for two and a half years. Can you narrow it down?"

Feeling their crazy captor's ire getting hotter, her anger and rage slapping him in the face, Buck worked hard to keep his heart rate steady, his muscles lax, and his breathing from giving away the fact that he was awake. For some reason, for some inexplicable purpose, he just knew the element of surprise was the only way he was going to save Freddie.

Damn, I hope I'm right...

"Of course, I can." The *tap tap tap* of what he instantly recognized as high heels on rock echoed through his mind. Zenobia was moving forward, leaving his side and getting closer to Freddie.

Breathe, Buck. Just breathe. Your mate is strong, smarter

than you ever thought about being, and a trained agent. She can handle this until you figure something out.

"But first," Zenobia hissed, the hate and disgust in her voice so thick he could've cut it with a knife, "I think you need a little reminder of who is in charge."

No sooner were the words out of her mouth than Buck heard the unmistakable static of a massive surge of electricity, immediately followed by, "Fuck, fuck, fuuuuuuuuuuck," coming from the direction of his mate.

Clenching his jaw, muscles shaking, it took every ounce of control he'd ever acquired not to roar. Not to break the chains holding him to some cold, hard wall in the bowels of the fresh hell created by some deranged yellow jacket named Zenobia. Not to save Freddie from being electrocuted.

I know that sound. I've heard it too many times. Felt the surge tearing through my muscles, eating away at my brain, nearly bringing my blood to a boil. I have to... I have to...

Biting down on his tongue to keep from roaring at Zenobia, something sharp, pointy, obviously metal, and incredibly small poked into the underneath side of his tongue. Unclenching his jaw as the surge of electricity ended and Freddie breathed, "I am so gonna kill you, Zenobia, and I'm gonna make it slow," Buck used the time their captor was filling the airwaves with her obnoxious, gloating cackle to drop his jaw and move the device to the top of his tongue.

Pushing it to the roof of his mouth, moving it back and forth, ignoring the blood dripping down his throat, a foggy memory emerged. Was it real? Was it a delusion brought on by the drug that big-ass dino had injected into his bloodstream? Was it because he didn't have the voice of reason—Harry—barking in his brain? Whatever it was, the recollection felt real. And it refused to stop playing through his mind. It was like an alarm clock he couldn't shut off.

"God, I ho-ho..." It was the same voice that had told him not to open his eyes just a few minutes ago.

Nope, not a hallucination.

Stammering and stuttering, gasping and panting, the deep rumble refused to be defeated. *"Fighting th-th-the bo-boss' pro-program. It's kill-kill-killing me...k-kill-ing us."* A loud gasp followed by another round of panting then silence, utter silence.

Ready to give up and take matters into his own hands, a loud sucking of air, something more than a gasp, way more, and so full of pain that Buck felt it in the very bottom of his stomach, slashed through the dark silence. *"Bite down. Bite down ha-hard. It will... That's what wi-will..."*

And the memory ended right there. Nothing else. No silent pause. No waiting for the next words. It was over, and Buck was back in the present with Zenobia screeching, "You always thought you were better than me, Winifred. Always won all the awards. Always graduated first. Fucking teacher's pet. They all loved you. Everybody loved *you!* They looked right past me—the brightest, smartest, most intuitive, most inventive, and definitely most beautiful—to fawn all over you."

Reaching her wailing crescendo, the shrill sound of her voice echoing back on itself, making it sound like there were at least four of her, Zenobia yowled, "But they will all see the truth. They will all see that you are evil, a cheat. That you stole everything you are from me! They will all—"

"What the fuck are you talking about, Zenobia?! Are you trying to live up to your old nickname? Did you get Zany Zenny monogrammed on your towels? I always knew you were insane, but this tops the nutball cake with whipped cream, sprinkles, and a big old cherry. You need a straitjacket and a strong prescription of lithium. I can help you with that. My best friend is—"

And just like that, the crackle and whir of electricity overrode every other sound. The rattle of Freddie's chains beat at his very soul. But it was the sounds his mate couldn't stop, the ones that her body had to make or it would simply spontaneously combust, the painful grunts and the squeaks he knew from experience were from her gritting her teeth and clenching her jaw so tightly her bones were about to shatter.

Thankfully, it ended almost as quickly as it had started. Even better, Freddie was not giving up. Sure, she didn't sound as strong, and there was a definite wheeze in her voice, but his mate as a fighter. She was a fucking superstar, and she was gonna float like a winged tree frog and kick the stinger right outta that yellow jacket.

"Oh, fuck you, Zenobia. Fuck you and the flower you rode in on. Go ahead! Kill me! Frame me for whatever you think you can. The FUC will see right through it. They will...what the fuck is that?"

That was it. Buck could no longer hold back. He had to know what was happening. Cracking his left eye—the one opposite the side Zenobia had been standing on—it was all he could do not to echo his mate's "what the fuck is that?"

Standing between the dais where he was chained to the wall and the spot about a hundred feet away from where Freddie was trussed in silver and sitting in the middle of a blue plastic kiddie pool with duckies on it, stood an exact copy of his mate. Same bright green eyes. Same gorgeous black hair. Same irresistible figure, with one glaring difference. There was a horrible, dark vacancy in her eyes. The lights were on, but nobody was home. The elevator did not go all the way to the top. It was *not* Freddie, only a shell, a copy... a fucking AI duplicate.

"Isn't she pretty?" Zenobia purred, stepping off the podium and walking toward the copy of Dr. Winifred F. Lightfoot. Running the back of her hand down the clone's cheek, she cooed, "All I have to do is program a little of your terrible personality and a tad of your incredibly lacking intellect and send her back to FUC to confess."

"But, they will never—"

"They will never what?" Zenobia shrieked, racing across the room and grabbing Freddie's face between her thin, skeletal fingers. "They'll never believe it's you? Hmmmm? They'll instantly recognize the ruse? Oh, Freddie, Freddie, Freddie," she poopoo'd, raising her free hand and snapping her fingers.

The sound of marching filled Buck's ears. He knew that sound. Instantly recognized it. "Dinos," he spat under his breath. "Muthafuckin' din... Holy shit on my shoes!"

Even through his barely open eyes, Buck could make out at least twenty of the dino soldiers. All exactly the same. Not one difference. Moving in unison. All their hearts beating as one. Right along with the copy of Freddie.

"Son of a bitch!"

Catching movement out of the corner of his eye, he saw the first one, the one he somehow knew had put the needle in his neck, move to the front of the line. Rage, utter hate, and contempt flashed in the dino's eyes, his strange elliptical pupils enlarging for just a split second. Then a spark of pain—no, check, agony—and then everything was gone. He was back to being a mindless drone.

"Well, kiss my ass and call me Sonny. That's it!"

Not waiting for another second, Buck rolled the piece of metal still balanced on the center of his tongue toward his molars. Opening his eyes wide, meeting Freddie's surprised, but oh so wonderful, gaze, he gave his mate a single wink, mouthed, "Hold on, hot stuff," and bit down as hard as he could.

10

He's alive! He's awake! Dammit, he's fuckin' gorgeous!

From one second to the next, a wave of energy, an explosion of power, a pulse that rivaled a small atom bomb, erupted from the vicinity of none other than Buck Blackthorne. From there, shit hit the fan in a glorious, chaotic, and absolutely fantastically effed-up fashion.

Zenobia shrieked, "No! No! No!" with her left arm flinging around like she was trying to take off or, at the very least, auditioning for air traffic control school. In contrast, her right thumb attempted to beat the stuffing—aka circuitry—out of tiny black remote control Freddie hadn't seen until that moment.

Buck, oh, gorgeous, handsome, hotter-than-any-man-ever-had-a-right-to-be Buck Blackthorne, the honey badger who made Freddie's heart go pitter-pat, pitter-pat, got all furry in the blink of an eye. At least seven feet tall, with muscles on top of muscles on tops of muscles, his chest, tummy, and everything else she could see was covered with coal-black hair she knew would be coarse to the touch and so sensual in all the right ways.

One jerk of his powerful arms and the massive brackets attached to the silver chains holding him to the stone wall were flying through the air. Left kick then right kick, and the ones shackled to his legs followed the same glorious path. In less than three seconds, her man was free and racing toward a running, well, more like stumbling 'cause she just couldn't walk in those heels, Zenobia.

And that was when Freddie's brain, or rather the part of her mind where self-preservation lived and the well-being of her mate stood alongside, kicked into gear. Shame, it was half a second too late.

Jerked out of the pool of water, chair and all, by the same dry, pebbly, scaly mauls that had captured her atop the mountain, this time with just the tips of its stubby, sharp talons touching her skin, she railed, "Put me down, you stupid son of a bitch! I swear on your black beady eyes that I will wear your guts for garters. I mean I don't wear garters, but I'll make one hell of a show out of—"

"Shut the hell up, Freddie." Bright's sass rang through the woman's mind. *"He's trying to help you. He's on our side. One of the good guys for heaven's sake."*

"Gutting you...like...a..." Words failing, head flying back, chin jutting into the air, her eyes meeting Dino Dave's, Freddie ended what would've been her best rant, most excellent bitch fest, and most spectacular threat in her whole damned life all rolled into one with a sheepish, "You're helping?"

"Yep," he growled. Making quick work of her shackles, the chains and the wires Zenobia had used to electrocute her, he produced her very own Trees Are People, Too T-shirt and shoved it into her hand.

Up on her feet, refusing to back away, needing the dino super soldier to know she would beat him to a pulp as soon as shake his hand, Freddie gave him a single sharp nod. "Thank you, but I'm still gonna kick your ass. That right there..." She gave a single, curt nod toward the crazy contraption she'd just escaped. "That was some serious bullshit, and you brought me here."

Not waiting for an answer, she dashed around the stupid kiddie pool Zenobia had used before stopping with one foot in the air and hissing, "That's it. That's what Zany Zenny was talking about. Holy crapola. She's still pissed about the senior games."

"The what?"

"No time," Freddie hollered to the dino super soldier, who was quickly bringing up the rear. "We gotta find Buck and your boss."

Two more steps and she stopped again, this time spinning on her toes and poking Dino Dave right in the chest. Throwing her thumb over the opposite shoulder, Freddie asked, "Umm, what's up with the bozo troop? Why are they just standing there like somebody took out their batteries? I mean, I know that life-size Freddie doll"—a creepy shiver she couldn't contain skittered down her spine—"has no giddyap in her get-along, but those dudes were climbing a mountain and blowing shit up just a little bit ago."

Smiling, the expression more than weird, especially with the view of his sparkling, pointy chompers, he said,

"Because somebody, namely Buck, took out their batteries."

"Huh?"

"Quick answer?"

Nodding frantically as she started to walk backward, needing to look the dino in the eye to be sure he was telling the truth, she ran as she snapped, "Go for it."

"I put a chip in Buck's mouth as the drug was taking him under and told him to remember to bite down. That chip sent out an EMP that shut down the boss'—"

"Zenobia…"

"Yeah, her programming, allowed me to break completely free, Buck to shift, and, in the process, turned off my copies."

"That's the short answer?" Freddie quickly queried as Bright groaned, *"Oh, my Lordy, be nice. We all know you're tough. You are Freddie. Hear you roar, blah, blah, blah. He's helping. Hurt him later if he gets outta line."*

"Yeah, what she said." Dino Dave smirked.

Snapping her head to the side even as she was turning to face front and pouring on the speed, Freddie warned, "Stay the hell outta my head. One smartass up there is enough. Do it again, and I'll stop right here, right now, and kick your ass winged-tree-frog style. Ya get me?"

Saluting as he ran beside her with a clipped, "Yes, ma'am, Freddie groaned. "You can call Bright that if you get the chance to meet her glorious green behind, but call me Freddie. Just hearing the word ma'am gives me hives."

"Yes, ma— Freddie."

With way more important things to handle, namely Zenobia Petalblast, Freddie put dealing with Dino Dave on her to-do for another day. Following the sounds of a fight, the glowing trail she knew was from Buck, which was right before her eyes, and Bright's directions, Freddie made a right, an immediate left, and another even sharper right in quick concession.

Flying through the enormous arched entrance of another massive cavern, Freddie skidded to a stop with Dino Dave right beside her. Blinking her eyes, needing to be sure she wasn't suffering the delayed effects of electrocution, the thought of laughing out loud literally danced through her mind.

Seeing Zenobia pointing a dinky remote at Buck and threatening, "I'll blow you up. I swear it. I'll do it," was priceless.

Of course, Bright threatened, *"If you do, I'm moving out and leaving no forwarding address."*

Declining to comment, Freddie shuffled to the right. Giving two sharp jerks of her head the other way, she smiled when Dino Dave got the message and mirrored her movements while heading left. Eyes back to her sexy honey badger, she instantly noted that the wide gray-white stripe she glimpsed on the very top of his head stretched across his back and went all the way to the tip of his tail, and oh Lordy, what a tail it was.

"Mind outta the bedroom, Freddie," Bright grumbled. *"There'll be time..."*

"Yeah, yeah, yeah..." Eyes darting across the room, she added, *"And just who the hell is the ginger-feathered chicken? Is she Team Badger Tree Frog or Team Zany Zenny?"*

Before Bright or, for that matter, Dino Dave—'cause she could still feel him in her mind—could answer, the six-foot-six Rhode Island red spread her wings wide, shoved her very long, very scary beak out as far as she could, and took off running at a high rate of speed right for Zenobia.

Flashing from short, thin woman to short, plump yellow jacket in the blink of an eye, Zany Zenny shot into the air like she'd been launched out of a slingshot. Something was wrong. Yes, it had been a long time since Freddie had seen her, but something about Zenobia's shift was all funked up. Her head was a weird mixture of bee and woman, not the usual partial shift mixture. Nope, this was an all-the-way deal, but it just wasn't right. And her midsection, well, it was okay in that her boobs were a damned sight larger than the human version of those delicate appendages ever had been. But what was horror-movie weird was the way what had been her pelvis, but post-shift was her stinger, had rolled forward from between her fifth and sixth legs and forced Freddie to scream, "Watch out. Her ass is poisonous!"

Knowing there were at least a million ways to better convey her message, Freddie breathed a sigh of relief when her honey badger and the big-ass hen understood. Watching then both spin and slide to escape the barrage of stingers Zenobia was firing, she called to Bright, *"Let's do this. After all, it's us the crazy bitch wants to kill."*

"And far be it for us to not be accommodating."

"Damn, I love it when you get sassy, Princess Raeanna Bree. It almost makes me giddy."

11

Green had just become Buck's favorite color. Never in all his years had he seen anything as beautiful as his mate in the form of her winged tree frog. Same gorgeous curves, same striking green eyes with ravishing red rings around the outside, even some of those same black curls on the top of her slightly flatter head, but every inch of glorious skin in vivid, eye-catching green with magnificent, flowing, rainbow wings.

"Spectacular," he and Harry breathed in unison, so lost in awe of seeing Freddie flying across the ceiling of the massive cave that they barely missed being shot with no less than four of Zenobia's poison stingers.

Ducking one way and then the other, ending up on his knees before rolling to the side and jumping right back to his feet, Buck hated that he wasn't up there with his mate. What if she got hurt? What if she got killed? What if…?

"What if you shut the hell up and pay attention?" Harry snarled.

Jerking himself out of the spiral his thoughts had

taken, Buck's eyes met Freddie's a split-second before she literally took a kamikaze run right at Zenobia. Expertly avoiding the flying stingers, cutting through the air like a fighter pilot, his mate slid right behind the yellow jacket's razor-sharp wings.

Watching Freddie's descent and her return back to the stunning, sexy woman he was already in love with, Buck was utterly confused. Not wanting to shift back, sure he would need Harry's long, impressive front claws, he couldn't deny the need to talk to his mate. To understand what was happening.

Then he smelled it. A sweet, almost tangy scent that burned the inside of his nose and made him need to sneeze. Poison! Tree frog poison. Damn it all to hell, Freddie was a genius. She hadn't missed her mark. Hadn't made a mistake by flying behind the yellow jacket. Nope, not his mate. She'd wiped her venom on Zenobia's back and let the sticky gel do the rest.

Buzzzz – buzz-buz-buzz-buz-buz-bubububuzzzzz

Searching for the deafening roar that sounded like an engine on its last legs, the honey badger's head flew back, his eyes locking onto Zenobia's spinning freefall toward the center of the cavern. Making it back to human form before she landed with a single thud, the yellow jacket shifter didn't even get the chance to groan before Freddie was there.

Back to human form from one running step to the other, Buck swung around to the opposite side of the prone perp, dropping to his knees. Hand on Zenobia's chest, he nodded to Freddie, so proud he could've burst when in a calm, relaxed demeanor he knew she didn't feel, his mate questioned, "Why, Zenobia? Why now? After all these years? Why come after me? After my mate? After my *coffee*?"

Biting his tongue to keep from laughing out loud, loving Freddie all the more because she was evidently just as addicted to coffee as he was, Buck gave his mate a quick wink when her gaze flashed to his. Eyes back to Zenobia, her wheezing cough and gushy gurgle making him cringe, Buck refused to move his hand, even as her broken sternum poked at his palm.

"Why?" Zenobia croaked. "Yo-You *cough-gag-cough-spit*..." Blood splattered on her drawn lips and pallid chin. "Be-because... *gag*... You-you always wi-win."

Hands slapping on the top of her head, her eyes open so wide Buck feared they might just pop right out and roll across the floor of the cave, Freddie yelped, "I what?" Sliding her hands off Zenobia's shoulders, her palms landing on either side of the yellow jacket's head, she got so close he wondered if his mate was going to head-butt the perp. Not that he would've blamed her. Hell, he wanted to do it himself. It was just that he was going to need to come up with one helluva reason if ever asked to explain why Zenobia had two black eyes and a broken nose.

But that wasn't what happened at all. Nope, not even close. As he'd already figured out from reading her file, Freddie showed ultimate compassion even to the woman who'd tried to kill her, well, at least she tried to.

"Have you lost your freakin' mind?" Answering her own question without taking so much as a breath or pausing the tiniest bit, Freddie rapidly rambled, her rage fueling every syllable. "Yes. Yes, you have. You need to be committed. There has to be paperwork unequivocally stating that Zenobia Petalblast is nuckin' futs, out of her mind, completely off her rocker, and never coming back. You… YOU…" She gave a sharp nod with her head. "You are crazier than 207,352 bedbugs, the number of those little biting beasts that can fit on the tip of your stupid skinny little finger. Do you seriously mean to tell me that you have spent all these years, faked your own death, created an army of dino super soldiers—?"

"Guards… *cough-spit-sputter*… *gag*…"

"Whatever!" Freddie roared, sounding a little manic even to Buck's loving ears but wholly justified, so he decided while letting her continue her rant.

Back to her original train of thought, Freddie railed on, "Constructed this…this …" Springing upright on her knees and flinging her arms open wide, she screamed, "Hive. It's a fucking Hive, Zenobia. You're a freakin' yellow jacket, and this is your hive. But you didn't build it to find a nice yellow jacket fella and have a shitload of little yellow jacket babies. OH NO! That would've made too much sense."

Palms back on the floor, her face right in Zenobia's, Freddie seethed. "You made it to house all this crap just to kill me." Head bouncing to emphasize every word, she snarled, "And to destroy my coffee. My precious, precious coffee."

"Wa-was th-th-the only way. *Cough-gag-spit* And so, is this."

Raising her hand and tapping the face of the thing on her wrist that looked like a watch from the thirty-first century, Zenobia smiled a bloody, gross grimace before closing her eyes and snickering. "I win."

"No!" Dino Dave bellowed, snatching a stunned, wide-eyed, slack-jawed Dusty and throwing her over his shoulder. Heading toward a tunnel Buck hadn't known was there, the soldier roared, "That's the self-destruct button. Run! Run! Run!"

Snatching Freddie off the floor and cradling her in his arms, Buck spun on his toes, taking off at a sprint as his mate demanded, "Take me back. Put me down or take me back. We have to get her. We can't leave Zenobia. She's got an escape hatch, a way out, something! I have to know why the hell she used wolfsbane! We can't go yet!"

Steps stuttering, trusting his mate, Buck was just about to make a 180 when the unmistakable sound of a C4 denotation whooshed past them, causing a ringing in his ears that reminded him of way too many times he'd been in the center of the blast. One right after another, a cascade of explosions rocked the floor beneath them, the walls all around them, and the ceiling over their heads.

"Damn, she's good," he shouted. "The charges are set like dominoes. One setting off another. Spiraling toward the center… the center… HOLY SHIT!"

"WHAT?!" Freddie screamed. "What do you know that I don't?"

"The main power source is at the center!"

"Shit! Shit! SHITSHITSHITSHITSHIT!" his mate roared.

The sound of her mind working at about a million miles a minute buzzing through his own, Buck wanted to listen, but saving their collective asses took precedence.

The rate at which the blasts were happening was cut in half with every earth-quaking explosion. There was no doubt that Zenobia was batshit crazy to the hundredth power, but Zany Zenny knew how to rig a demolition.

Pouring on the speed, holding Freddie as tight as he could, the honey badger suddenly recognized where he was. Making a beeline for the same steel ladder Harry had used to get them down into the hole, Buck ran faster than he ever had in all of his already long life.

"Just make fuckin' sure we both get a helluva lot older," Harry demanded.

"I gotcha covered. You just be ready if I need ya."

Ten feet away, every molecule of the ladder in his sights, Buck pushed off the rock floor, hit the bottom rung with the balls of his feet, and grabbed the bar just above the top of his head with his right hand. Loving that Freddie reacted so quickly and in the perfect way, her arms wrapping around his neck and her legs around his waist, Buck scrambled up the ladder, through the opening, and out into the cool evening air. Not letting his mate go even when she loosened her grip and let her legs swing free, he didn't miss a beat.

"Feet, don't fail me now!"

Following Dusty's yellow-throated-warbler call, he answered Freddie before she could ask the question, roaring into her mind. *"That much C4 is gonna light up this entire mountain. We can't st—"*

But whatever he was about to say was lost as an eruption to rival Mt. St. Helens threw dirt, plants, trees, everything within a radius he had no time to calculate, cutting through the air with damn near supersonic speed. Holding even tighter to Freddie, wishing he was the one with the wings, Buck grinned from ear to ear when Harry's long, hooked claws erupted from the tips of his fingers as his hands became furry with tough, thick pads.

Twisting his body, dropping his right hand from around Freddie's waist, Buck used every ounce of his paratrooper experience, only this time in reverse, to get them out of the blast. Still in midair, his hang-time the shit of legends, he spun his mate onto his back and barked into her mind, *"Hold on tight. Don't worry about strangling me. I can breathe through anything."*

"You got it, ace," came her clipped reply, making him smile all the more. Dammit, Freddie was one of a kind, and she was all his.

Extending his arms as far as they would go, Buck drove his nails into the face of the small mountain. His feet immediately joined the partial shift, the shorter but sharper claws sticking out of his toes did the same. Climbing the side of the foothill was more comfortable, even better with Freddie on his back. It was just the way they were meant to be, stopping crime, kicking ass, saving the day—*together.*

"Yeah." Freddie chuckled, reminding Buck that she could read his mind. *"We'll get T-shirts. Honey Badger Strong. Tree Frog Fabulous. We Ain't FUC'N around."*

Chuckling as he hooked his claws on the flat surface of the peak of the mountain, Buck gave a single, concentrated jerk with every ounce of power thrumming through his body. Drawing his knees to his chest as he sprang into the air, Buck hit the ground on the balls of his feet, the tips of the claws of his front paws keeping them upright.

Standing tall, he didn't have time to ask Freddie how she was before his fantastic winged tree frog jumped off his back, ran around to his front, and jumped right back into his arms. Arms once again around his neck, her legs so tight around his waist that their hips were almost fused in absolutely the best of ways, Freddie slammed her lips to his.

Kissing him like a woman possessed, just the way he liked her, the tip of her tongue slid along the seam of his lips, demanding entrance. Opening completely, Buck gave as good as he got. It was everything he'd ever imagined being with his mate would be—and so very much more.

Lost to the passion, wondering how Freddie felt about very public displays of affection—aka sex on a mountaintop with the world below exploding—Buck was just about to ask when the clearing of a throat and an all-too-familiar chuckle had him pulling away.

Smiling with more than his share of male pride at the sight of Freddie's kiss-swollen lips and her heavy-lidded eyes, he winked. "To be continued."

"You know it, Badger Man."

Reveling in the fact that Freddie didn't loosen her grip or try to get down as he turned toward Dusty, who was still chuckling, Buck pretended to be irritated as he scoffed, "Something amusing, soldier?"

"Yep." The Rhode Island red laughed out loud. "Funny as hell. And I ain't callin' you sir."

Laughing along, Buck had just opened his mouth to give as good as he got when Freddie launched herself out of his arms. Hitting the ground running, his mate made a beeline for the dino soldier standing off to the side, hands behind his back, at ease, for lack of a better description.

Not slowing down, her steps not faltering in the slightest, Freddie bent her knees, shot her five-foot-something height to the wall above the dino's almost seven feet and roared, "Paybacks are a bitch."

Seeing her balled-up fist only when it was flying through the air, Buck fell absolutely completely and totally head over heels in love with his mate when her knuckles connected with the dino's jaw. Head snapping to the side, forced to take several steps backward to stay on his feet, the dino shook his head once, twice, three times.

Rubbing the blooming red splotch on the side of his short, scaly snout, the soldier gave Freddie a single nod. "It's the least I deserve."

Stalking back and forth in front of him, the hem of her T-shirt flashing Buck with the bottom of the wonderfully creamy globes of her very pleasingly plump badonkadonk —words he picked right out of her mind— on every deliberate step, the honey badger had to remind himself that it was not time to claim her as his own.

Ready to act if the dino made a move to lay a single finger on his mate, Buck was instead shocked to his very core as the soldier added, in a sad, solemn tone, "I have the answers to your questions." Pulling a memory stick from the pocket of his camos, he came damned close to pleading, "All I ask is that one of your scientists see if they can turn me back. Find the man I used to be buried in the fucked-up mess Zenobia created of my DNA." Slamming his fists to his chest, the thump so loud it could be heard over the rumbling of the aftershocks below, he matter-of-factly finished, "Turn me back into a T-Rex iguanodon shifter or put me out of my misery. I do not want to live like this any longer."

Letting his head fall forward, precisely two seconds of utter silence ticked by before the dino looked back up, smiled a crooked grin, and, looking at Freddie, chuckled. "And I like the name Dino Dave, but my mother called me Alexander. Alexander Anatoli."

Spinning on her toes, eyes as round as saucers, Freddie threw her thumb over her shoulder and gasped. "Son of a bitch. I know this guy."

Arriving right on cue and a few minutes earlier than she would've liked, three FUC Black Hawk helicopters descended all around them. Leading the charge was Miranda and Chase, instantly taking Alexander into custody, getting him cuffed faster than she could move.

Racing after them, with Buck hot on her heels, Freddie shouted, "Go easy! He's one of the good guys."

Stopping midstep and in perfect unison, the couple's heads also snapped to the side at exactly the same time before Miranda challenged, the voice of her big bad bunny heavy in her tone, "You wanna run that by me again? Are you sure you shouldn't let the doc take a look at your head? We heal shit pretty quick, but concussions can be freaky things."

"Oh, ha, ha, ha, very funny," Freddie scoffed, stopping next to the bunny. "I swear..." Holding up the memory stick, she continued to explain. "I know this dude. Something in his eyes seemed familiar from the first time I saw him." Tilting her head to the side and nodding, she pursed her lips and wiggled them back and forth for half a second. "Of course, he was trying to capture me, I was trying to kill him, and in the process, he drugged me and delivered me to Zenobia, but..."

Head popping back up, she looked at Alexander then back to Miranda, reaching to grab Buck's hand just because she could *and* she really needed the added support of somebody who had been there. "There was something...right in there"—pointing at the dino super soldier's face, she narrowed her eyes then nodded—"that told me this guy was not all bad. He was a victim of circumstance."

"Well, while I trust you, Freds," Chase grumbled unconvincingly, "how about we leave the cuffs on and the clips on those vicious-looking pinchers of his until we get your buddy here back to the safe house and have a word with ... What did you call him?"

"Alexander Anatoli," Freddie quickly answered at the same time that the scaled soldier responded, "Dino Dave."

Bursting out with laughter, sure a large part of it was just her body, mind, and Bright's way of expelling a bit of the massive amount of adrenaline racing through her veins, Freddie inhaled then went right back to explanation. "I'm pretty sure his DNA, what's left of the real stuff he was born with, will show him to be Dr. Alexander Anatoli, distinguished paleontologist, archeologist, and dino shifter."

"You knew there was a dino shifter out there?" Matt Firestone asked, appearing on her other side.

"I did not," Freddie admitted, more than a little embarrassed but doing a damn good job of hiding it, given recent events. "I guess I always had my suspicions, but Dr. A here kept his secret really well." Slowly shaking her head, she added, "And we were digging in 120-degree weather in the middle of some godforsaken desert. I freely admit that my brain was otherwise engaged. I was young. I missed it. Sue me."

"Force of habit when you're as old as I am."

"Yep." she nodded thoughtfully, thinking back over some of the things he'd said all those years ago and the sheer amount of knowledge he had on all things ancient. She should've known or at least guessed. "I can only imagine." Back to Miranda and Chase, she inquired, "So, if you can rush the DNA test, I would—"

"I'm on it," Delilah chimed in, appearing out of the smoke and crowd of people.

"Where the hell did you come from?" Freddie asked, gladly accepting a big, warm hug from her bestie while snickering. "I swear, it's a fucking FUC convention up here. Who's minding the shop?'

"Don't you worry about it," Matt reassured. "I have it on good authority that every agency in the alphabet soup that makes up organizations like ours is anxiously awaiting your report, Freddie." Not waiting for a response, the dragon turned to her mate. "And as for you, cadet..." The last word was growled.

Instinctively taking a step forward and then to the side, shielding her mate from the professor, really experienced FUC Agent, and dragon shifter, Freddie got as far as, "Everything that happened was my fau—"

But Buck was too quick, not that it surprised her at all. Wrapping his arm around her shoulder, using the move as a way to scoot her to the side and step forward, her honey badger stood tall. "Yes, sir. I acted on my own accord, and I will—"

"Be graduating early and taking your place as a FUC agent immediately. Consider yourself FUC'd." Matt chuckled. "Mates!" With his snickers turning to laughter, he added, "Y'all are something else." Pulling the ringing phone out of his pocket and glancing at the screen, he advised, "I have to take this" Looking at Buck, he added, "You might want to stay close. This is your brother-in-law, and I have no doubt Shauna, too."

"Great," Freddie's mate groaned. "Can you tell sis that I already left? Please? I'll owe you big time. Free drinks at the Sundowner for a year."

"Add coffee to the list and you got a deal." The dragon snorted with a wink, answering the phone as he turned away.

"We have to get him to the safe house." Chase spoke up with a sideward glance toward the dino. The DIC is waiting."

"The who?" Buck sputtered, his laughter getting the best of him and making Freddie giggle as she explained, "Direct Interrogation Coordinators, highly trained agents with the ability to extract information humanely—for the most part."

Reaching for Chase's outstretched hand, she followed his pointed gaze to the memory stick still firmly between her thumb and forefinger as the grizzly inquired, "They're gonna need that, don't cha think?"

"Oh, shit, yeah, but…"

"But you wanted to have a look at it first?" Miranda

nodded, handing Freddie a small FUC-n-GO, the newest, most compact design of a handheld computer she'd ever seen. "Use this to copy the info. You can replay it on the screen. It's—"

"New and from Willem." Freddie snickered. "Damn, that man never stops."

Doing as the bunny instructed, Freddie watched the percentage of download increasing when she remembered she was waiting for results and asked, "Hey, what about the DNA?"

Eyes meeting Del's, she laughed out loud when the doctor shook her head. "Girl, did you doubt me? Or yourself, for that matter?" Holding up the handheld DNA synthesizer, Del nodded. "And you are right again. As if there was any doubt." Eyes clouding with a sadness Freddie had seen before, one that said the cruelty of people was something she would never understand, the doctor confirmed, "There is little of the original DNA that hasn't been altered, but it's there, and this man is indeed Dr. Alexander Anatoli."

"And if those little beauties are there, we can do our damnedest to fix them, to return the doctor to his original, brainy self."

"If anyone can do it," Dino Dave, aka Alexander, replied hopefully, "it is you, Freddie Lightfoot." Swinging his head to Chase, the dino nodded. "I am ready to go. You have my full cooperation and undying gratitude."

Watching them walk away, Freddie instinctually and comfortably leaned into her mate, and then it hit her— what she'd almost forgotten. Words flying out her mouth, she shouted, "What about the wolfsbane, Dino Dave? Do you know why Zenobia used it? What was it for? Did she modify it? Do I need to synthesize an antidote?"

Turning his head to the side, his eyes narrowed as they met hers, renewed hate flaring to life, the dino snarled, "To trap you. This was all about trapping you, Freddie. Zenobia cackled like the lunatic she was when she had the idea. Said you couldn't stand things that didn't fit, unsolved puzzles. Knew that if for no other reason than to solve the mystery, you would come here, and then she would have you. That was also the reason for the explosion and the debris that could be seen from the sky. I am so sorry."

"Son of a bitch!" Freddie swore. "And the award for craziest bitch in the universe goes to…drumroll please… Zenobia Petalblast." Meeting Dino Dave's eyes, she forced a smile. "Not your fault, dude. I'll see you as soon as I can."

Looking up at her sexy-as-hell honey badger, Freddie smiled a goofy grin and whispered, "And as for you, I have a question. Who is the Rhode Island red? Better not be an old girlfriend. I have a jealous streak you would not believe. Heck, I turn green when I need to, and like another awesome emerald-hued hero, I have the authority to say you wouldn't like me when I'm angry."

All he wanted to do was take Freddie back to the swamp, strip her down to her gorgeous naked body, and have his wicked way with her. He'd literally thought about it so many times and hard enough that even Harry was tired of hearing it. *"Son, you just need to go all Neanderthal on your mate. Grab her up, throw her over your shoulder, and head out. Once you're in the air, what can she—"*

"Jump out of the plane because she has wings."

"Well, shit, I forgot about that." Harry sighed. "Okay, I got nuthin'."

And neither did Buck. His amazing mate was hearing none of his well-crafted, expertly delivered reasons. She wanted to stay at the site of the explosion. Needed verification that Zenobia was well and truly dead. Had to know that the copy of her had been destroyed.

Freddie had to know. Had to see it with her own eyes. Otherwise, in her own words, "I'll be flippin' like a fish, constantly lookin' over my shoulder and wonderin' when Miss Cuckoo Crazy Pants is gonna pop up and try to kill us all again. Or..." And this was where her finger flew up between them and wagged in sync with her words. "I'm gonna open the door and find myself staring back at me. Nope, not going anywhere till I know for sure."

So, Buck joined the dig. Twelve hours in and no closer to finding anything but pieces and parts of dinosaurs, lab equipment, and electronics, he climbed out of the massive crater, stalked over to where Freddie was standing, and put his hands on her shoulders. Looking deep into her eyes, he announced in a tone that left no room for debate, "We're going home."

Holding up his finger when she tried to speak, he kept right on going. "To *my* house. That crazy bitch is dead. Your doppelganger was destroyed. You know it." He tapped a tempo in sync with their beating hearts on her chest. "I know." Throwing his thumb over his shoulder, he confidently added, "They all know it, too. You need to sleep." He laid a tender kiss to her forehead. "I need to hold you." He kissed the apple of one cheek and then the other. "And I need—"

Putting her hands on either side of his face, Freddie pulled his lips to hers. Kissing him with all the passion he felt mixed with a shit-ton of her own, his mate whispered into his mind, *"We're sleeping on the plane, 'cause when I get you alone, all bets are off."*

"Damn." Buck happily sighed. *"I love you, Freddie Lightfoot."*

"I love you, too, Buck Blackthorne. Even more, if you have lots and lots of coffee at your place."

"Oh, baby, I gotcha covered."

True to her word, Freddie slept almost all the way

back to the swamp, her head on his lap, her hand holding tight to his. He couldn't look away, didn't dare let his eyes close. Sure it wasn't a nightmare that ended in a dream, knowing it had all really happened, Buck simply refused to take his eyes off her. He had his mate right where he wanted her, and heaven help anyone who tried to get in the way.

"Hey, boss," Dusty whispered. "How's she doin'?"

"She's great." Recognizing the sappy tone of his voice, the honey badger just couldn't care. It felt good, really good, so much so that he hummed, "She's fuckin' awesome."

"I heard her ask about me." Chuckling as softly as a Rhode Island red from the deep south with a wicked sense of humor ever could, Dusty quipped, "My jaw 'bout hit the ground when she asked if I was your ex."

"Me, too." He snickered. "But she doesn't know either of us very well. Okay, she knows me, 'cause of the whole mate thing, but not even Freddie could've dug that far into my past in that short of a time. I guess it makes sense."

"Yeah..." Dusty's answer trailed off, making Buck turn his head to look her in the eye.

"What's up?"

"Oh, nuthin', I was just... Well, it's that..." Hemming and hawing, something the Rhode Island red never did, the honey badger bit his tongue and waited. Something was up with one of his oldest and closest friends, and he wanted to be there for her in any way that he could without pressuring her to talk before she was ready.

Then, like a switch had been flipped, Dusty's head

popped up, she grinned from ear-to-ear, and asked, "So, what the hell was the deal with the blue plastic kiddie pool? I know there's a story there. I heard you ask your girl, but I was stuck talkin' to that lady agent and missed the answer."

Deciding that his friend would tell him what was up when she was ready, Buck snorted as he nodded. "Seems that when Freddie was in school with Zenobia, there was an obstacle course in gym class for some kind of senior thing. Being who she is, Freddie tried her hardest to be the best, to win the race. So, doing that weird hippity-hopping kinda running thing anybody would have to do to get through the big tractor tires, she was neck and neck with Zenobia. Then she got a little ahead, about half a tire width, but not enough for her likin'.'"

"Oh, my Great Goddess, she didn't." Dusty laughed.

"Yep, she did," Buck nodded, snickering at the mental image he'd seen in Freddie's mind. "Our girl here tried to hurdle the last tire. As she said, 'I am, after all, part tree frog, figured I could give it a little extra hop without shifting.'" Stopping to laugh, he shook his head and continued, "Well, the toe of her tennis shoe got caught on the deep tread at the edge, she started falling, and in her effort not to faceplant, she reached for the only thing she could…"

"Zenobia," they both whisper-laughed in perfect unison.

"Yeah." Freddie's scratchy, sleepy giggle entered the conversation. "And wouldn't you just know it, the next obstacle was the water trap." One hand went limply in the air, making a half-hearted air quote before flopping back onto the seat. "As I'm sure you guessed, there was a line of those blasted kiddie pools, and Zenny and I landed ass over tea kettle in ours."

Yawning so wide and so long then going silent, Buck thought Freddie might have fallen back to sleep. He rubbed lazy circles up and down her arm, smiling when she finally finished with, "When she said that she'd make me pay for embarrassing her in front of the whole school, I thought she was just mad. Hell, teenage girls get mad all the time and get over it. Guess that shows you what I know."

"Naw," Dusty said. "How the hell were you supposed to know she was crazier than a pup in a hubcap factory?"

"Yeah, I guess you're right." Looking up at the hen, Freddie asked, "Buck says you built this jet."

"Yes, ma'am, I did," Dusty proudly answered. "I saw the one you built, too. Sorry, it went up in all that mess back there, but I bet you can build another, even better."

"I was actually thinkin' about that."

Moving his arm as his mate pushed upright then placing it around her shoulders when she cuddled close, he wasn't surprised at all, actually proud as any man could ever be, when Freddie went on. "How about you come to work with me?" Holding up her hand as Dusty inhaled to speak, his mate hurriedly added, "Think about it. You and I together with my genius buddy, Willem? What the three of us don't know about aviation hasn't been discovered. And you're a shoo-in for the Academy. Heck, bet you beat Buck's record for the shortest time as a cadet."

"Hey." Buck tried to act affronted but only ended up chuckling as he looked at his friend.

Smiling brighter than the day she beat Russell

Wollingham, the wolverine they went to high school with, in the all-state wrestling finals, Dusty nodded with such gusto that her messy braids danced all around. "Yes. Yes. Yes, ma'am. I'm all in."

"Woooohooo," Freddie whooped. "And I promise no one will ever tell you that you can't fly your own plane ever again."

"Hey, I heard that," Delilah hollered from the cockpit, the humor evident in her voice. "I'm only following protocol. Your man there said to get you to the swamp as soon as possible, and I thought this was quicker than giving each and every one of you the twenty-four-hour follow-up examination, which would've held us up for at least another twelve hours."

"I'm shutting up," Freddie jokingly barked, complete with about half a salute.

"Yeah, that'll be the day." Dr. Weathersbee laughed out loud. "Buck, you better invest in noise-canceling headphones. Your mate tends to rant when she gets goin'."

Before he could answer, Dusty hooted and snorted, even slapping her leg. "So does the boss." Both hands jabbing the air straight in front of her chest, all her fingers pointing at Buck and Freddie, she chortled. "A match made in heaven."

Lowering his lips to Freddie's, Buck stopped right before they touched, playfully ordering, "Dusty, don't you think the doc could use your help in the cockpit?"

"Roger that, boss." The Rhode Island red giggled. "Roger that."

Buck's home was amazing. Nestled in the best part of the swamp, built on stilts, the perfect little cabin in the trees, Freddie was sure she'd died and gone to heaven.

Unfortunately, they'd just made it across the threshold and closed the door when in walked his mom, two brothers, his sister, and the biggest friggin' dragon shifter she'd ever seen. He made Matt look like a runt, not that she'd ever tell *him* that.

Nervous, knowing she looked like something the cat dragged in and worried they wouldn't be thrilled with her lineage, tears literally filled her eyes when Buck's mom hugged Freddie without hesitation. The stunning, short, curvy, older woman with blonde hair and mischievous blue eyes wasted no time in announcing, "Welcome to the family. You are just the best-lookin' little thing I ever laid eyes on," and Freddie was overjoyed.

Then it got even better...

When Janice finally let go and stepped back, she

added, "And I hear you're smart as a whip, tough as cob, and fierce as any honey badger around. I couldn't have picked better for Buck if I'd been asked." Leveling her gaze and furrowing her eyebrows, the matriarch of the Clan grumbled toward her son, "Treat Freddie right, or I'll jerk a knot in your tail, ya hear?"

And that was how the next hour went. Everybody in the Blackthorne Clan, as well as Shauna's dragon mate, Abe, accepted Freddie with open arms and hearts, and the best leftover ribs she'd ever sunk her teeth into. They even made coffee, three pots of strong, black java with cinnamon, just the way she liked it. Everything was so much better than anything she'd ever imagined. She almost hated to see them go... but, just almost.

No sooner had the door shut and Janice hollered, "We'll see ya tomorrow. Breakfast at nine," from the ground below than Buck swept Freddie off her feet and made a beeline for the bedroom.

Thankful that she'd been able to shower in Dusty's plane, and super glad her mate wasn't expecting lacy underwear and a sexy bra, she was swept away as Buck had her naked on the bed and him down to just his boxers in a matter of seconds. Unwilling to miss the show and knowing firsthand how fast her mate could move, Freddie couldn't take her eyes off her honey badger.

Watching him make a show out of losing his boxers had her heart racing and her pussy wet, and then he climbed onto the bed, crawling up her body, and all Freddie could do was gawk at his gorgeous body. She'd known he was built. Hell, his muscles had muscles, but to see it all right before her and know he was all hers was nothing short of mind-blowing. As his erection touched the top of her thigh, all thoughts of anything but consummating their union like bunnies getting ready for Easter Sunday fled from her brain.

Her hands couldn't stay still. She touched his chest and ran the back of her hand across his nipples, giving him a sexy chuckle as he shivered and growled low in his throat. She'd waited long enough. Freddie needed her mate more than she needed her next breath.

Sliding her hand between their bodies, she wrapped her fingers around his erection, bowing her back when he dipped his head and sucked as much of her breast into his mouth as would fit. Sucking her hardened nipple between his teeth, Buck tasted and teased as her fist worked his cock into hard perfection.

Pulling away with a gasp, lust and love shining brightly in his beautiful blue eyes, Buck growled, "I need to be inside you. I need you." Kissing her jaw, nipping at her neck, and lavishing her shoulder with his lips, he whispered, "Only you, Freddie. Only you."

"Yes...oh yes, yes, yes," she gasped, letting go of his erection and digging her nails into his shoulder as her amazing honey badger balanced on the hand that was by her head and slid the other slowly up the inside of her thigh.

Teasing her already wet curls, Buck's forehead touched her as he slipped first one and then another finger inside her pussy, sighing. "Oh, god, you are so wet, so ready. I want to have your taste on my tongue. I want it everywhere. I want the whole world to know I belong to you and only you." Panting, a glorious sheen covering his olive complexion, he gasped. "But that will have to wait. I have to be inside you—right now. No more waiting."

Working his digits in and out of her slick pussy, Buck looked deep into her eyes as his thumb began to taunt her swollen, throbbing clit and he purred, "But first, come for me, Freddie. Scream my name. Wet my hand. Come, my love, let me feel how much I turn you on."

As the last word crossed his lips, her fabulous honey badger, the one man she'd been waiting for her whole life, squeezed her clit between his thumb and forefinger. In the blink of an eye, Winifred F. Lightfoot experienced the first-ever screaming, mind-blowing, almost-passing-out orgasm of her life. Not a single one, either with another guy or all by her lonesome, had ever compared. Everything she'd ever heard about being with her mate was true and then some.

It was fabulous, life-changing, and further confirmed that Buck Blackthorne was the man for her. Kissing her lips with all the passion and fire she could feel boiling between them, Buck slowly pulled his fingers from her still quivering body and, with a sensual roll of his hips, slid just the tip of his erection inside her.

Raising his head, capturing her with his smoldering gaze, Buck slowly, inch by glorious inch, pushed into her body. Filling Freddie so that she had no idea where he stopped and she started. It was like flying for the first time.

Wrapping her legs around his waist, taking just a little

bit more of her mate into her body, she gasped as the blue of his eyes began to swirl, and in the most sincere, heartfelt tone, Buck murmured, "I love you, Dr. Freddie Lightfoot-Blackthorne. I love you more than I ever thought possible. To the bottom of the swamp to the top of the mountain and everywhere you go, I love you, and I'll always be by your side."

Pulling back until she thought they would be separated, Buck stopped just in time and held perfectly still. Staring into not only his eyes but his soul, Freddie saw forever, and it was fucking awesome.

Then he drove back into her body. A man possessed with her pleasure before his, Buck created a rhythm that became frantic and more wonderful with each thrust.

All rational thought ceased. Her nails dug into his shoulders. She spoke in languages yet to be discovered and loved her man like there was no tomorrow. Tiny orgasms shot through her body as the tips of his canines scraped the tender spot where her neck met her shoulder.

Hips thrusting to his, Freddie's fingers dove into her mate's hair, fisting the blond curls and holding him tighter to her heated flesh. Opening her mouth, she tried to beg. She wanted to plead. Hell, she would've been happy to utter a single intelligent word, but her brain was in its happy place and refusing to help in the slightest.

Leaning back, Buck looked at her with beautifully hooded eyes and asked, "What is it, my stunning winged tree frog? What can I do for you?"

The glint in his eye was mesmerizing. He knew what she desired but wanted to hear her say it. Needed to hear the words. It was the sweetest, most endearing thing ever. Slowing his thrusts, he purred, "Say it, my love, tell me what you want."

"B-bite me, d-damn you." With her hips refusing to be still and her body needing what only Buck could give her, Freddie inhaled as deeply as she could and demanded, "Bite me, B-Buck. Dammit, I l-love you. Now, make me yo-yours."

Smiling with male pride, a look that would've pissed her off on any other man but looked really damned good on hers, her mate resumed the amazing rhythm that made her body hum at the same time that he kissed down her neck, licked the spot he'd already been teasing, and said, "I love you, Freddie, and now, you'll be mine forever."

Canines sliding through her flesh, holding tight to her pounding pulse and shaking muscle, Buck's bite sent a fiery thrill of love and passion tearing through her body. Screaming her release as Buck held on tight and emptied his seed into her body, Freddie knew she was as close to Heaven as she'd had ever been. Floating back to earth, she whispered into her mate's mind, *That's a trip I wanna take again...lots.*

"Oh, darlin', you have no idea the plans I have for us."

Hours later, and after a few more trips to Buck and Freddie's Happy Place, she was cuddled up with him, loving the feel of having someone she belonged to and who belonged to her, when Buck kissed the top of her head and whispered, "I have a present for you."

Raising her head, Freddie shoved her hair over her shoulder and waggled her eyebrows. "More than what we just did? You sure we shouldn't hydrate?"

Barking with laughter, Buck snorted. "That was not a present. That was a necessity. If you hadn't agreed to let me mark you and love you for the rest of forever, I would've exploded all over the damned swamp."

Patting his chest and rolling her eyes even though she was secretly thrilled beyond measure, Freddie playfully scoffed, "You would've been just fine. Remember, one of my degrees is in medicine."

Moving so fast the room spun and she ended up on her back with a sexy, turned-on honey badger looming over her, Freddie's heart did that silly little pitter-pat thing as Buck kissed her until she was breathless and starry-eyed all over again. Pulling back long before she was ready and winking when she groaned and tried to keep him where he was, Freddie Lightfoot's amazing mate rolled to the side, taking her along for the ride.

Stopping only when they were face to face with her left hand in his right, she was instantly lost in his eyes. So captivated that she almost missed the feel of something cold sliding down her ring finger.

Snapping her head to the side, all she could do was gasp. "What the…? For me? How did you…? Son of a gun, I'm gonna cry, and tears aren't my thing. I just don't… But I think I just might…"

Shaking his head, Buck looked more than a little scared as he stammered, "H-Happy te-tears, right?"

Looking away from the most gorgeous ring she'd ever seen—a platinum band set with seven perfect stones, one for each color in Bright's wings—Freddie closed the distance between them, pressed her lips to her mate's, and whispered directly into his mind, *"Yeah, they're happy tears, ya big goofball."*

"Good, 'cause sad, unhappy tears from you just might kill me."

Groaning low in his throat as their kiss grew more passionate, their legs tangled, and their bodies heated again with love and passion. She knew that was how it would always be for them. Crawling on top of her mate, Freddie reluctantly pulled back from their kiss and looked down at the man she knew she would love forever.

Smiling as he put his hands around her waist, sat up, and began kissing down her neck, she grabbed his shoulders as his erection grew hard between them. Pushing him back ever so slightly, Freddie gave her mate a saucy wink and purred, "Oh, no, big guy. It's my turn to do the biting."

Rolling his hips against hers, his eyes swirling with love, Freddie's very own mate wound his fingers in her hair and held her close as he whooped, "Oh hell yeah, now that's what I'm talkin' about."

Yep, no doubt about it. Buck Blackthorne was the honey badger for her, and that made one very special tree frog happier than she ever knew possible.

All was more than right with Freddie's world. How could it be anything less? She had Buck, she had Bright, and, thank heavens, she had coffee. Now, that was a happily ever after worth fighting for.

THE END

To find out more about these books and more, visit Worlds.EveLanglais.com or sign

up for the EveL Worlds newsletter. If you haven't already downloaded the **free**

Academy intro (written by Eve Langlais) make sure you grab it at

worlds.evelanglais.com/wordpress/book/fucacademy1!

Hey, y'all! I'm Julia Mills the *New York Times* and *USA Today* bestselling author of the Dragon Guard Series.

I, without a doubt, admit to being a sarcastic, southern woman who would rather spend all day laughing than a minute crying. Living with my two most amazing daughters and a menagerie of animals keeps me busy, but I love telling a good story. Now that I've decided to write the stories running through my brain, life is just a blast!

My beliefs are simple. A good book, along with shoes, makeup, and purses will never let a girl down, and no hero ever written will compare to my real-life hero, my dad! I'm a sucker for a happy ending, and alpha men make me swoon.

I'm still working on my story, but I promise it will contain as much love and laughter as I can pack into it! Now, go out there and create your own story!!! Dare to dream! Have the strength to try EVERYTHING! Never look back!

I ABSOLUTELY adore stalkers, so look me up on Facebook, sign up for my newsletter and follow me on BookBub.

XOXO Julia

Find all Julia's stories on her website!